SPIN A SILVER DOLLAR

The Story of a Desert Trading Post

Spin a Silver Dollar

THE STORY OF A DESERT TRADING-POST

By Alberta Hannum

Illustrated with Color Reproductions of the Work
of the Navaho Boy Artist

LITTLE NO-SHIRT

(Beatien Yazz)

1946
New York: The Viking Press

PUBLISHED BY THE VIKING PRESS IN NOVEMBER 1945
PUBLISHED ON THE SAME DAY IN THE DOMINION OF
CANADA BY THE MACMILLAN COMPANY OF CANADA LIMITED

SECOND PRINTING NOVEMBER 1945

THIRD PRINTING FEBRUARY 1946

FOURTH PRINTING MARCH 1946

THE ILLUSTRATIONS IN THIS VOLUME HAVE BEEN REPRODUCED
IN FULL COLOR BY THE REEHL LITHO CO.
THE TEXT HAS BEEN SET IN LYDIAN AND GRANJON TYPES
AND PRINTED IN U. S. A. BY THE HADDON CRAFTSMEN

To Sallie's Father

ACKNOWLEDGMENT

The author wishes expressly to thank her friends the Lippincotts and Dr. Donald Weeks for their generous lending of Beatien Yazz originals reproduced in this book.

ILLUSTRATIONS

SPIN A SILVER DOLLAR

CHAPTER

1

WHEN the Lippincotts had to give up their trading post at Wide Ruins for a while, because of a man named Hitler, Jimmy kicked a skunk. Jimmy was the son of their Navaho handy man, and so shy that he never said more to them than yes and no—although he always said that twice.

"Yiss—" The first time it would come only in a whisper. Then the little boy would clear his throat and try it again, a little louder. "Yiss—" and duck his head, to hide a smile as shy as he was.

He never talked to the two young white people who, in an airy moment, had come into his part of the Arizona desert with its canyons and junipers to run the old Indian trading post there. But he followed them everywhere. He followed them literally—clumping along behind them in the heavy yellow shoes all Navahos love. And he followed them figuratively, out of his world into theirs.

Jimmy is the name he was given at the little stone schoolhouse, half a mile away from the trading post, at the top of the hill on the other side of the wash. But he had another—Little No-Shirt, his nickname. All Navahos have two names, and those who go to school have three. They have their school name, their real tribal name with which they are born, and their nickname. This last they go by almost altogether. Navahos do not like having their real names known. They're proud of their names and don't want them bandied about carelessly. They don't want their good names worn out.

This was one of the small constant run-ins with the Navaho mind which kept trading with them an uncharted business. And their stubbornness about refusing to allow their real names to be used was a trait especially confusing to the system of bookkeeping Bill tried to install in the old store, whose main attraction had not been system.

The Navahos, from the beginning of their generations, have been known among themselves as The People—an assurance which let them blandly ignore the threat of the Spanish sword, and arrogantly overlook the fact when they were supposed to be under Mexican dominion; and later kept an American army of over three thousand men, for eighteen years, at an expense of some $3,000,000 annually, marching purposefully against them, only to march baffled back again. So it is hardly surprising if they are not particularly interested in modern American business methods.

But as they came to know that the new young trader had a sense of humor as caustic and keen as their own, and that they could trust him—when they brought him a sack of wool he'd bang it down on the counter to hear how many rocks were in it and to shake out some of the sand, and then adjust his scales only as much as was right and proper, not cheating them—they indulged him in his notions for a while. They obediently took away with them their half of a ticket he would give them when they'd put an ancient silver bracelet or fine leather saddle in pawn, and dutifully bring the ticket back again when they came to redeem their wares. They went along with him in this—until they began to notice that after they'd redeemed their property, he'd tear the ticket up. Thereafter they didn't bother. Why should they keep a ticket with their name on it just for him to tear up? And it never was their real

"—with a delicate sweetness that haunted the mind a long time."

name anyway. So the books, defeated, read Mouse's Brother, Old Trap Mouth, Harold Clark, Frank Run in the Springtime, Big Shorty.

Sallie and Bill soon found they had nicknames themselves. Bill's was Burned Hat, and Sallie's She with the Hair that Is Red. Bill got his the time the store blew up, and Sallie's was obvious, from the quality of its brown. Little No-Shirt came by his through the artists from Munich who visited at the trading post. The artists came in the spring and, fascinated, stayed until the fall. That summer they grew so interested in the Indian boy and his artistic possibilities that they tried to teach him what they themselves had learned. It was an almost disastrous attempt, for Jimmy had a way of his own that he had to go. But since the Navahos knew that both the child and the visitors painted pictures, and since one of the visitors was a sun addict who went without his shirt, the little boy became known as Little No-Shirt.

Little No-Shirt in Navaho is Bea Etin Yazz. Finding he was using that name, Sallie wrote it down for him once, so he could see how it looked when spelled out. Thereafter he faithfully used all the letters she had put down for him, but he would rearrange them as the mood struck him. But essentially Beatien Yazz came to be the signature down in the righthand corner—the pencil obviously held in a painstaking grip, and the resultant scrawl with a childish uphill slant—on all the pictures that he painted.

It was a matter of ever-fresh amazement that so real a little boy—frequently showing up with a black eye and always with his hands dirty, unless Sallie caught him first and then he washed them up to the wrists, on the inside—could paint the pictures that he did. They were in water color, and often with a delicate sweetness that haunted the mind a long time. Yet sometimes they carried such a sharp uppercut that the observer would look at them uncomfortably and say, "That kid's too good."

Jimmy's pictures were of the animals he knew on his desert —the rabbit and the mouse, the skunk and the wildcat and the deer, and most of all the wild horses of the hills. He painted animals, but animals with human expressions, and always his paintings had some emotional carry-over from things that happened around the trading post in the nearly four years the young white people had it.

So that a worldly way of life was recorded pictorially by a child of the primitives, with the child and the adventure growing along together.

"The animals
he knew
on his
desert

...recorded pictorially by a child of the primitives"

BEATIENYAZZ

CHAPTER

2

ALL that the Lippincotts had known about the Southwest, before, they had loved—the wild, deep, free feel of it, the quiet power of it. But just what there was about the old Wide Ruins trading post itself which had struck them the first time they had seen it, just passing by, they could not have said exactly. Actually the place was only a lot of neglected old stone buildings, set in a high shallow bowl of the desert. But the bowl had been so gently irregular as to seem almost carved out by hand, and despite their outward dilapidatedness, the stone housings looked set into it solidly. There had been a quietness and solidity to that first passing of the place which stayed with them all summer.

That was the summer which they spent, newly out of the University of Chicago, in the Park Service at Canyon de Chelley. Their quarters were just across the road from the McSparrons' trading post there, and they began spending more and more of their spare time around the store. Cozy McSparron's father had been associated with Indian trading, and Cozy knew as many of its tricks as any white man ever will. The Lippincotts were so captivated by the ins and outs of it that they came to know a little about the business themselves.

At the end of the summer, as they were getting ready to leave that part of the country—regretfully, because they had had more fun there without trying than they ever had before

—the McSparrons said, "Why not buy a trading post, and stay?"

Sallie and Bill laughed with them at the idle wildness of the idea, for a minute. The next minute they were doing a quick double take and saying, "Well, why not?"

The more they thought about it, the more running a trading post seemed to have all the essential ingredients of the kind of life they were beginning to think they would like to live—an independent one, in a part of the country they enjoyed. And with the growth of the idea, they found that the presence of the old trading post at Wide Ruins, which they had passed that first day on their way into the desert, had been in all their revolutionary thinking throughout that summer.

Cozy McSparron told them Wide Ruins was owned by Peter Parquette, the oldest trader on the reservation, although he took little interest in the business any more. In fact, he'd taken Wide Ruins in on a bad debt, from a woman who had run it wearing jeans and a brace of pistols. From what they could hear, the internal workings of Wide Ruins were as much on the down-go as its outward appearance. Still, the thought of it held.

From an Arizona guide book, they found that by actual mileage it was 18.6 miles from the town of Chambers. The town of Chambers was a water tower and a system of railroad switches, an express office and a store. But the Chief, which flung past back of the store, would stop there if a Wide Ruins passenger insisted upon it. This unscheduled stop always made the prospective visitor very unpopular with the train crew, from the engineer to the porter, and the other passengers would crane out the windows curiously at their fellow-traveler being let off out there in the middle of nowhere, beside a water tower, wondering whether he were socially unfit, or just sick.

Mail also was thrown off at Chambers and brought on by anyone who happened to be going on into the desert—a salesman, or a visitor—and in the meantime while it waited for delivery all its magazines and newspapers and post cards were interestedly read. Telegrams could be called in to the Chambers "post office"—a flank of pigeonholes at the back of the store—and the first chance the storekeeper got he would take the telegram half a mile down the road to the express office. The express office had no telephone. An incoming telegram lay in the express office until somebody from the store happened down that way, or else news of it was relayed up to the store, and then it was sent out with the regular mail.

Once a New York shopper sent Sallie a coat on approval. The coat sat around Chambers for quite a long time, and, not hearing, the shopper grew worried and wired. It was only by the sheerest accident that the particular telegram ever got into the Lippincotts' hands at all. The telegram had been given to an old Indian of the Wide Ruins neighborhood, to take back and deliver, from his venture to the edge of the reservation at Chambers. It was his first sight of the world outside, and a big Greyhound bus barreling past had so captured his imagination that he came back toward Wide Ruins only as far as the first hogan, where he knew someone lived who had wider experiences with the out and beyond than he. His friend fixed him up with a note which gave him a point of destination and reason for travel on the bus. So instead of coming on to Wide Ruins, he betook himself back to Chambers, and hailed the next Greyhound. As it happened Bill had gone to Chambers for the mail that day, and noticing an Indian having trouble trying to board a bus, recognized him as one from Wide Ruins.

With the big bus snorting and champing at the delay, all the passengers fascinated, but getting mad, too—the little old Indian over and over again would climb aboard and get thrown off. But before the bus could start up and get away he would be back on and have to be put off. Bill went to see what the trouble was. Although the Navaho could speak no English, he kept shoving under the driver's nose a piece of dirty paper which he had clutched firmly in his hand, on which his friend had inscribed, "This going to Winslow."

"He wants to go to Winslow," Bill told the driver.

"But he's got to pay me first!"

Bill explained this to the Indian, who then dug into the back pants pocket of his levis and brought forth a Bull Durham sack. Levis are of tight cloth, and the pocket small, and it took him some time to wrangle the sack out. The sack was tied with a string, knotted with many knots, which he undid knot by knot, while time passed, and the big bus waited. The fare was a dollar and seventy-five cents, and finally, nickel by nickel, dime by dime, he got it out—then climbed happily aboard, and the bus roared off in frustration, leaving Bill with a telegram which the Bull Durham sack also had produced, wondering what had happened to a coat sent to Wide Ruins on approval.

Regardless of its irregularities, Chambers did offer contact with the world. The highway the big buses traveled was a main one, Route 66, the only transcontinental highway which stayed open all year long. That, however, was more than could be said of the Wide Ruins road leading to and from it.

According to the guide book, the road in to Wide Ruins from Chambers was an "improved dirt" one. They were to find that the "improved dirt road" in March was frozen ruts, in April deep mud, and by May had drifted so full of sand no one could get through it. In fall it was too muddy and slippery for comfortable travel, and in winter they dug their way foot by foot with a shovel, hoping for a thaw, and then when the thaw came, the road turned gumbo. In any season it washed out altogether with every rain that came. However, on dry days in summer it was a fine road.

Their own first remembrance of it was a brown sand road that wandered up hill and down and went loose on the curves, wound around through juniper forests and now and then went past an Indian house. These little round hogans built of red cedar were not set together in villages, but each one separately, wherever its owner saw fit, because the Navahos believe there is room enough for everybody on this earth and people should live wherever they choose. And each hogan always had space around it, as though the people who lived there wanted room enough to walk around without having to draw in their elbows, and wanted air to breathe. Sometimes, though, the space was brought closer by a fence of tangled juniper branches. But both the juniper fences and the low cedar hogans were so much a part of the earth that the newcomers to the country would almost miss these habitations unless they turned to look again.

It was high country (the guide book said an average of about 7,000 feet) yet it had a lulling quality to it, a sense of give and flow. Even the dark green junipers had more spread than spear. There had been a reservation of judgment as to that first 18.6 miles off the highway into the desert, that early summer they first had traveled it. And then they had topped a rise, and below, in the shelter of a shallow valley, had been Wide Ruins.

From the practical point of view, whatever the seasonal condition of the road leading into it, the location of the Wide Ruins trading post was an advantageous one, so far as accessibility went. It was not so easily reached as to encourage a passing tourist trade, which they did not want. On the other hand, it was not so remote but what they still could have touch with the world they had known.

More, they found there was good reason for that handmade appearance of the shallow bowl which sheltered it. It *had* been carved out by hand—by the Old Ones, or the Anazazis, as the Navahos called the ancients. From an archeological source book, they found that Wide Ruins was one of the largest Pueblo sites of the Southwest, and that in its original days as a dwelling place it had been called Kintiel, or Broad House. In fact, the trading post still was known arbitrarily either as Wide Ruins or Kintiel. Early maps of it showed square stone rooms, two stories high, terraced into the side of the hill and looking down upon an open court. Excavators from the National Geographic Society had estimated, from datable beams in the ruins, that its stone walls had been laid up sometime between 1264 and 1285 A.D.

But of vital importance in that desert country, they further unearthed the fact that the site had been chosen by those ancients because of a deep spring there, which still was in use, and whose original masonry was still intact.

And that first feeling of immediacy which sometimes comes between people and people, or between people and places, sprang to excitement when they heard the Wide Ruins trading post was for sale. But directly on the heels of that news, catching up with their excitement at its height, was the word that it already had been sold. It was then, when they knew it was not there for them, that they realized just how disappointed they were. It was like approaching a post box, with that quickening which comes with the anticipation of a wanted letter, and then finding nothing in the box but the shadow of its emptiness.

Still, they stayed on, and throughout September considered two other posts which happened to be for sale on the reservation at that time too. One was in a dark nook of the Black Mountains, and offered the attraction of a bathtub. The

bathtub, however, was of the old-fashioned variety which sat
high on claw feet, and for some reason known only to its
owners its height had been further increased by setting it on
a wooden platform the same size as the tub so that you got
into it with difficulty and out at the risk of your neck. Furthermore, only cold water ran into the tub, and that a vague
dribble which seemed hardly worth the bailing out by hand
which had to be done, since no provision for a drain had been
made. Besides, the store there was dark as a cave, and dirty,
and the whole thing too remote.

The next place had no tub, but it had a shower. The trader
himself had designed it, and was infinitely proud of it because
it was a hot-water shower. He'd run the pipe through the
kitchen stove. The slightly disconcerting drawback to the
arrangement was that he'd run it right on out through the
kitchen wall to a place outside by the woodpile. It was the end
of a long dusty day and Sallie had trailed the trader's wife
gratefully at the cordial offer of a shower. Then she stood
uncertainly, looking up first at the iron pipe bent blandly
ready above her, then at the scant protection of the woodpile,
and then at a group of men a few yards away in the horse
corral. But her hostess, at the hesitation, heartily reassured her.

"You just go right ahead like you was in your own house."
With that she wheeled, cupped her hands, and charged the
world in general, "Everybody on their honor! Bath's in use!"

The store there was adobe, with a flat sheet-iron roof, and
dark as the inside of a hat. But neither the lack of conveniences
in the living quarters nor the modernizing that was needed
in the business end of it would have held them back at either
place, had their hearts really been in the search.

September can be a time of violence on the desert, but also
it can have its smackless times. And these particular September
days were being pale ones. Perhaps it was because it was ex-

ceptionally cool that September, but both sun and shadows looked thin. A dunness had seemed to slide into everything.

And then, in October, they heard that it had been a mistake —that Wide Ruins had not yet been sold!

Wide Ruins had neither bathtub nor shower. The store there was even darker than the other two had been. Its floor was flagstones laid in the dirt, its counters old and heavy, its rough board shelves unpainted. The store adjoined the house with all of it on one level, except for unexpected steps up and down into this and that of its wandering rooms. There were bad places in the roof, with birds skimming in and out. All the house ceilings bowed, and were braced here and there with chicken wire. All the walls were covered with plasterboard and painted a depressing battleship gray, except for one wall in one bedroom, and it was baby blue. It developed that in all the two-hundred-foot frontage of the place the only thing centered was one heavy lintel under one low gable. Lest convention get the better of him, however, the builder had off-centered the deep-cut little window under the gable. No one window was exactly like another, and each one wavered a little in its top and bottom dimensions. But somehow the very awkwardness of the place seemed an assurance of its underlying soundness.

But still, they didn't want to show their draw to the place too early in the deal.

"We'd have to put a new roof on right away," criticized Bill.

Mr. Parquette was hurt. "I don't see why. That roof only leaks in a few places."

There was a good deal of dickering. Mr. Parquette offered to throw in the furniture—that is, the kitchen furniture—the wood stove, whose oven door did not quite shut, Sallie noticed, and the chairs and a wooden table that was so big they subsequently had to take it out through the roof. He firmly refused, however, to part with the living-room furniture. It was the curlicued overstuffed variety, with the springs shooting up here and there out of the overstuffing. They demurred, but finally agreed to let him take it. On their part, they refused to include as store stock the pile of frightful Navaho rugs stacked up at one end of the living room.

But in the end the bargain was made, and Mr. Parquette, under the bandanna he wore knotted at four corners to make a hat, was radiant. It seemed that, along with two old men who had been living there with him, he was about to satisfy a lifelong ambition. Now that Wide Ruins was off his hands, he and the old men were going in together to buy a car and go see Mexico.

Everybody was pleased, and as a friendly wind-up Mr. Parquette asked the new owners to stay and eat dinner. It was nearing noon, but just having seen the kitchen they said no thank you, they weren't hungry. Mr. Parquette was disappointed.

"Not even a cup of coffee?"

It seemed, then, the thing to do. "If it won't be too much trouble—"

"Oh, it's no trouble," Mr. Parquette assured them. "We've got some on the back of the stove left over from yesterday."

But fortunately, as he was bringing the pot to the table, he tripped over a bad place in the floor that had been patched with a piece of packing box, and spilled the coffee and had to make some fresh. Sallie and Bill sat at the big kitchen table and had coffee and a dish of plums which the men stewed up —two of the men bustled around, one cooking and one serving them, while the other just sat and beamed on them, holding his false teeth in his hand!

That was on a day in October, in 1938. The Navahos call October the Back to Back Month—when one division of time turns its back on another and starts out in a new way. The passing of time is not measured by numbers on a calendar by the Navahos. Rather it is gauged by the remembered force of storm, or the look of spring again. It is marked by the feel of change, and by the things that happen to people.

When the two young people came out from the house that day, with Wide Ruins theirs, they came out into a stillness. But it was a stillness that rang in the ears, and it was windless. An old cottonwood by the house, and a younger one over by the road, both stood quiet. There was not a stir to the tamarisk bending along one side of the house yard. There was not a sound, and not a sign of anyone about. For a moment they seemed the only people anywhere.

And then a shadow fell on the sand in front of the store doorway. The shadow fell clean and clear. A little Navaho boy, in faded shirt and blue overalls, was coming out. His heavy yellow shoes made a clump on the old wooden doorstep. It was a loud sound in the quiet, and he stopped, in embarrassment, at the white people looking. A slight child—slight like a string of rawhide, with something about him that made them smile a little, involuntarily. He almost smiled in return. Then he frowned fiercely.

At that they laughed outright, and the cottonwoods that had been standing high, and the tamarisks that were bending still, waiting for the touch of the wind, felt it come.

The next time they saw the child, he was a ways off from the trading post. They had walked out to see what the desert immediately around them was like. From the trading-post yard itself there was just a brown sand road coming down a sharp hill from the direction of the highway. The view was brief in that direction. The other way it was longer. On the far side of the post, going on, the road dropped into a wash and out again, and up a long hill past the schoolhouse. From the top of that hill, beyond, lay the mountains.

That day they walked out as far as the wash, and turned, and followed it a ways. The rocky wash sides grew intimate with dried yellow cliff roses as they went along, and with junipers bending over the cliff edges under the windy weight of sun upon them. And then, in a sheltered lee of the rocks, they came upon the petroglyphs.

They had seen something of these rock drawings in other parts of the desert—figures of men and animals cut into stone by people who had been there before, and left their record. At Canyon de Chelley they had seen the drawings known as Padres on Horseback—the Navahos' record of the White Strangers, as they had called the Spanish, who had come to conquer them. By the late 1700's the Spanish had given up the task as being beyond them, but the unconquered people had put the effort down.

Always a keenly acquisitive race, cleverly taking whatever appealed to them in other races and adapting it to their own, even this practice of leaving their mark in rock probably had been picked up from a people before them, for the Navahos are not an old race, comparatively speaking. They are a parvenu race and a mixture something as America itself. The Navaho racial beginning is placed at less than two thousand years ago, and the cuttings in the rock the Lippincotts came upon that day were done by a race which preceded them. They were imprints of hands—fine hands, of infinite delicacy. They were the hands of the Basket Weavers, whose time was about that of Christ.

The wash broadened out and curved, and around a wide bend in it were more of these rock drawings. But these were later, from the Navahos who had followed the Basket Weavers.

And although the Navahos had used the same medium as the Basket Weavers, the petroglyphs they subsequently had left of their own were quite different. They were the simplest kind of line drawings. Angular, almost childlike, and yet with great freedom, and a strange force to them. One of these which Sallie and Bill found that day was of a man, and beside it another of an animal which might have been a sheep or a goat.

Then, starting back toward the trading post, cutting across the wash at a different place, they saw the little boy again. He was sitting on the sand, scratching out a picture on the flat side of a rock with a sharpened smaller rock.

The picture, when they went to look, was that of a horse. There was nothing outstanding about the drawing itself—any child of eight or so, which seemed about his age, could have done it. But that the little Navaho boy was doing it in stone, as his people before him had done, interested them.

When they asked him his name, he turned his dark little head around almost backward to hide a smile which was his only answer to their interest. But Mr. Parquette told them he was Joe Toddy's boy—he thought his name was Jimmy. And the first time they went to Gallup, which was the nearest shopping center, for supplies, a drawing book for Jimmy was on the list.

As they went to get in the car for the trip they found a little old woman in long draggling skirts and a blanket wrapped around her like a shawl, standing by the car, staring at it with bright eyes. She was Little Woman, the oldest woman of the Toddy clan—the oldest woman of any clan anywhere, Sallie was sure. But Little Woman had that bright-eyed interest in everything, and fear of nothing, which some rare old people have. And she seemed so captivated by the car that they took her along.

They went whooping along with the top down, and every

time they hit a bump Little Woman would start sailing out, and Bill would have to grab her back in. But with every mile her delight in the car picked up, and all at once she gave out an ejaculation like the shout of the heroes. That is the way all Navaho chants start:

Ho, ho, he, he!

Little Woman was old and wrinkled, and light as a feather, but she could sing! All the rest of the seventy miles to Gallup she sang "God My Grandfather," from the Yeibichei chant, at the top of her lungs.

Ho, ho, he, he, haya, aya,
Ho, ho, he, he, ho, ho, haya, he—

By the time they reached town she was so thoroughly enchanted by the car that she wouldn't leave it. They parked on one of the main streets, and Little Woman sat in the red sports model convertible in state. She climbed up and sat on the back of it like a spectator at a horse show, her blanket folded neatly now and set squarely on top of her head. Little Woman sat and watched the world go by, without it seemingly occurring to her that the world was a little curious about her as it passed.

It was a conglomerate lot on the streets of Gallup that day— Indians from the near-by Hopi and Zuni tribes, as well as the Navahos, distinguished from each other by their dress and the way they wore their hair. There were Mexicans in the crowd, and ranch owners and bean growers and cowboys, and travelers changing trains there—people going through on their way West, or stopping off on their way from the West to the East. Gallup has been a meeting place for Americans in the Southwest almost since America began bearing the name.

The Navahos particularly used to follow desert trails across mesas and through canyons to come together at this "place by the bridge" as they called it then. A scattered, nomadic people —but they came together in war; an imperious people in those days, meeting to swoop down on one of their enemies—their more sedentary neighbors the Pueblos, the intruding Spaniards, the Mexicans with whom they never got along. It made little difference which. The Navahos were men of war who, by such impartial preying, had grown from a strong handful to a power to be considered. And within the memory of people still living—Little Woman could remember it—they had met here at this place by the bridge to strengthen themselves in defense against the subduing force of the United States Government.

Gallup still was a center for the Navahos in a way—a distributing center. All the traders from the reservation brought in their pinion nuts, pelts, jewelry, blankets and wool, and shipped them out from here. In turn, Gallup was the center for the wholesale houses, from which traders bought their supplies. There was still a raw, frontier feel about the pink-slag and tin-front town of Gallup.

All the way back to Wide Ruins, Little Woman sang the Yeibichei chant. Sallie had found some crayons and a box of water colors and a painting pad in an art shop for Jimmy, and although his small handsome face lit up with all his shy pleasure, he accepted the gift silently.

But a few days later on the kitchen table they found the drawing book mysteriously returned, and it was all filled.

The pages started out with childish line drawings. The first was of the Puberty Ceremony for boys. It was merely a straight line-up of figures—a small one representing a child, and three larger ones in crude masks who were the gods. In the next picture, the line was broken. There was action to it—the boy was trying to get away. In the third he was bent to receive the lash of the whip one of the masked gods was raising above him, and there was a suggestion of fear and curiosity in the boy's uplifted face. These still were not particularly unusual drawings in themselves—except for the fact that they knew Jimmy had not gone through the Puberty Ceremony because of his age, and because in the real ceremony the gods unmask, to show the child they are not really gods, only their elders trying to teach children discipline. So the little boy evidently had a trend for drawing things he heard talked about, or caught a suggestion of, as well as from actuality.

Some of the pictures, as the book went on, were in crayon, and some in water color, and sometimes both crayon and water color in the same picture. Some of the pictures were so awful they were funny—like the one which had big footprints making great headway across the scenery, and two wolves, with the saliva streaming, hot on their trail. There was nothing subtle in the idea back of that. But the footprints were brown, and the wolves were brown, and as though this balance of coloring at a venture had struck some note in the child, the next picture had hulks of three brown buffalo like shaggy shadows on tan. On the last page those colors were washed dimly in the bent figures of men wearing hides, who might have come out of the caves of time.

The shy, silent return of the drawing book filled for them was the Lippincotts' first present in that part of the country they were choosing as theirs—a country so rawly new still, and yet so untouchably old, and all of it very simple.

CHAPTER

3

TO MAKE Wide Ruins livable, a great deal needed to be done. Toward this they let the store go as it was for a while, and concentrated their efforts on the house.

As Bill had mentioned to Mr. Parquette the day they were dickering for the place, their first move toward renovating was to tear off the roof. Mr. Parquette still could not understand their reasoning about this. He and the two old men had not left yet. After all, despite the fact that now they were free to fulfill a lifelong dream, when it came right down to it they couldn't bear to leave Wide Ruins. So they took the overstuffed furniture over to the weighing house by the sheep corral on the other side of the road and camped, and looked on disapprovingly at the changes being made. Mr. Parquette, it seemed, had had a very good system about those leaks in the roof. For the big leaks he used buckets, and for the little ones saucepans. He obligingly showed them which was which, but they took the roof off anyway.

Since they had to have help with all they were planning to do, they hired the first Indians who came along. As it happened the crew all belonged to the Shorty clan, which was the worst bargain the hirers could have made, as they realized afterward. The Shorties were not bad Indians—it was just that they had leisure down to an art. It was a wrestle even to get them started. With the Shorties, it was one thing to know there was a job to be done, and quite another to do it—they didn't want to rush into those things.

Then one morning when a couple of them were just sitting on the roof, as though if somebody yelled they'd not jump till Tuesday, there came shuffling up through the yard, like an important bear, a newcomer to the scene.

He was a stocky figure of a man in a black satin shirt and several pairs of overalls—evidently on the theory that no two holes in any of the series would hit at the same place. A musty red headband held back his wild shoulder-length hair, and there was a racy light to his eyes. Here at last was an Indian who showed a little spark of life to the body—although he overdid it. He started bossing the Shorties around, and the Shorties laid down their unused tools and quit.

Left with the field his, he stood looking after them with his leathery forehead wrinkling imposingly. There was unconsciously great sadness in that face, and great humor, too. He looked like Don Quixote. Still, they wanted to be sure.

"You aren't another one of the Shorties, are you?"

He was indignant. "Here'ss Joe Toddy!"

At that they regarded him with even greater interest. This, then, was the father of the little boy who drew the pictures.

"Do you think you could handle this job for us, Joe?"

They came to know later that Joe had a passion for being in the spotlight in the white people's world. At any appearance of a visitor to Wide Ruins, they could always look around and count on finding Joe draped dramatically against the landscape. Now at the success of his ruse for calling their attention to him, there came a happy flash of big, very white teeth, and his black eyes narrowed and glinted.

"Here'ss Joe," he said again, and all but raised the flat of one hand by way of announcing that now their troubles were over.

He tore into the roof and started ripping off its odds and ends of sheet iron and tar paper and board patchings as though he were in a knife-throwing contest. He had the roof off in record time—and came down off the job with his enthusiasm for work all gone. But by that time they had worked up an enthusiasm for Joe, and kept him on as general handy man around the place.

They saw Jimmy around occasionally. But unlike his father, who went prominently strutting through their world without understanding it, they seemed to catch their glimpses of Jimmy only as he was disappearing out of sight around a corner someplace, taking that grin they were coming to look for with him. And he never spoke to them. But now and then they would find a present on the kitchen table—an odd piece of colored paper with a picture on it.

From the colorless chiseling on stone which they had first found him doing, the little boy had come quickly into a love of color—as though it had been there all the time, back in, on the other side of the edge, just waiting. And from trying one color against another, as he had first done when Sallie had brought the crayons and box of paint, now he was experimenting with backgrounds of color.

A little scrap of yellow-green sun paper had a brown lizard sprawled on it. And on an odd piece of black wrapping paper which had come into the store, he did a gray night skunk. Once it was something from their own mail which was given back to them. He'd rescued a wedding invitation from the wastebasket. It was of that particular white that wedding invitations are, and on the back of it he painted a creamy rabbit.

Somewhere he had found another piece of white paper but this time so assailing a white that one little bear had his paw up before his eyes, as though against a blinding sun. An opposite little bear was on all fours, going after a fallen red oak leaf, the same color as the little bear's pleased tongue. In the middle a bigger bear, taking time out to enjoy the fall, too, was reaching up a clumsy paw for a butterfly.

Seeing his pleasure in different colors and qualities of paper, whenever Sallie came upon an odd piece of it thereafter she would save it for him. Bill had fixed up a drawing table for Jimmy at the back of the store, in the ware room, and Sallie would lay her offering on the corner of it for him. He would pretend not to see it. He would slide his eyes toward it as she put it down, and then go on working at what he was doing. Perhaps the new piece of paper would lie for days untouched. He would even draw papers out from under it, without seeming to notice it was there. Then one day he would pick it up, and make some direct, infallible use of it.

Jimmy gathered his idea for color out of the desert around him—and color was there. It was in the trunk of the cottonwoods, chalk white against the china-blue sky. It was in the very sand—enough wildness and redness in it to make it beautiful. He drew his ideas for colors from things as they were, but he used them arbitrarily.

From the first time they saw Wide Ruins, they had known a charm to be in the place. But they kept being freshly surprised at each new revelation of it as they went along.

The natural living-room ceiling, once the roof overhead and the plaster board and chicken wiring underneath were off, disclosed an unexpected slope. It climbed gently upward a long way from the windows at one end of the room, then, at the last minute, dropped steeply down to the high little square ones at the other. And it was beamed with twenty-four slender pine logs, set the short way across, which gleamed like honey when they were cleaned and oiled.

The stone walls, which had made so easy a line against the sky from the outside, proved to be in some places three feet thick, some places two feet, laid up without rule, as though some early mason had worked his way down them as he saw fit. So that the living room when it was stripped of its beaver boarding was narrower at one end than the other, and its side walls bulged out like a Buick.

They plastered the walls in cream-colored adobe, which afterward held the glow of the firelight in its unevenness. An Indian plasterer put it on by hand, with the flat of his palms, in swirls. Swish, swish—and as he plastered he sang. Some archaic song with words he didn't know the meaning of, it seemed, when Sallie asked. It was an individual song. He owned it individually. If he gave it to anyone else he couldn't sing it any more. It was pitched in the minor, a nasal and rather quiet song. It sounded like doves under the eaves. Then every once in a while he'd stop his private ditty and go beat vigorously on the tom-tom he'd brought along.

On the whole, this particular period in the reconstruction of Wide Ruins was one Sallie and Bill were glad to see passed, however. It had been warm as spring when the Shorty outfit had sat on the roof edge dangling their moccasins in a delicious delay of action. Even all the time Joe was industriously tearing off the roof, the wind had been a soft one, wrapping around the house like a rope, like a silk rope, and birds had sung in it. But immediately the roof was off the wind picked up and turned suddenly cold. Had the three old men not still been in the weighing house, Sallie and Bill would have moved over there. As it was they camped out where they were, with four walls and no roof and a snow beginning to fall—wet flakes of it that stuck to things.

"Leaving the known to fare forth into the unknown, in search of a dream at once superb and sublime—an allegory of every phantom that the high heart of man has ever pursued" looks romantic in the printed record of it afterward. And perhaps in earlier days there was a glorious fascination in conquering that new world and the savages who were in it.

But in November of 1938, with winter falling early, glorious was the wrong adjective for their brushes with the present red-faced savages. The old roof was off, but, in that country where they were finding nothing could be forced, the Indians were so long in getting around to putting a new one on that by the time the house finally had covering again, its stone walls had become so thoroughly damp the plaster wouldn't dry. The wet plaster gave off a damp penetrating chill and Bill's cold turned into influenza. At first he wouldn't believe it. It was impossible to be sick when there was so much to be done.

"It's just that you naturally feel like hell the first hour in the morning," he argued, when he tried to get up and couldn't. "If you'd just stay up all night so you could go right to work in the morning, and skip this first hour, you'd be all right."

But he wasn't all right. The one modern convenience the trading post had boasted when they had bought it was a telephone. "Handiest thing in the house," Mr. Parquette had said proudly. It would have been especially handy, then, to have called the Ganado hospital twenty-five miles on across the desert, where the nearest doctor was that night. Ordinarily that would have been the simplest of any call to make from Wide Ruins, because even to get Chambers eighteen miles away, the connection had to be made through Ganado, who called the head agent at Window Rock thirty-five miles on farther, who put the call on the main line to Gallup some forty miles off in the other direction, who then called the fifty miles back to Chambers.

This night, perhaps because of some mix-up in the wires from the blizzard outside which was cutting across the desert on a horizontal wind, Sallie could not get Ganado. Once, frantically hanging on to the line waiting for an answer, someone said cheerfully, "Victorville"—which is in California. She started over, and the next time got El Paso. Finally the connection went through, but they couldn't hear her at the hospital.

During all this there had been vaguely mixing in with the smell of the wood fires she was trying to keep high all over the house against the dampness of the plaster, an underlying duller smell which grew heavier and thicker. As Sallie hung up the receiver in a last futile attempt to get a doctor, it was to the awareness that a wing chair she had pulled up close to the living-room fire was wreathing itself in its own smoke. A coal had snapped free of the fire and lodged in the upholstery and the chair was burning up from the inside.

Bill, who had been in the bedroom adjoining the living room, deep in the sleep of stupor that goes with flu, floundered up to the smell of cloth burning, rushed to the door—to see Sallie forlornly pouring water down a smoldering hole in the wing chair, out of a small crystal pitcher.

"There's a whole bucket of water on the stove!" exclaimed Bill.

"But that's *hot* water!"

It was quite true there was a deep and ancient spring at Wide Ruins, as the guide book had said, and that it still was in active use. But to use it, they had to go down the masonry steps the ancient ones had put in some thousand or so years ago and bring it out by hand. It was not piped into the house. Furthermore it was icy, as water would be from that far down. Hot water had come to be something to be respected.

Bill looked at her. Then he picked up the chair and strode out into the blizzard with it. He followed with the bucket full of water, poured it all on, and the chair promptly froze solid.

Later they sat huddled under blankets around the fire, having whiskey and water and aspirin, and Bill a great many shrimps. "Do you think," asked Sallie uncertainly—considering the diet of soft-boiled egg and tea he had been refusing listlessly all day—"do you think that you ought to have shrimps?"

"It isn't the things you *should* do in this world," said Bill moodily, "that keep you going. It's the things you shouldn't —I hope—"

The untimely violence of the first snow passed, leaving only a reminder of it in a lay of white in the road ruts. But it was a warning of the real winter that was coming, and Mr. Parquette and his two chums decided that if they were going to get to that "land where the summer follows the summer," as the Navahos call Mexico, they'd better get started. On the day of their departure Sallie discovered that the term "western hospitality" was more than a well-known phrase: it was a matter of course. She had twenty-one people that day for lunch. There were the three old men and all the ranchers in that part of the country who had come to see them off, and added to that host were two men who were lost.

The latter were travelers who were on their way to see a friend in the government service at Window Rock. It was strange country to them and they willingly enough had picked up a Navaho who was going that way, taking it for granted he would know his own territory and guide them through. They had gone plowing off across the desert and after hours of hard going found themselves at Wide Ruins instead of Window Rock. All desert roads look alike, especially when they're bad, and somewhere they had taken a wrong one. They turned to the Navaho who was riding with them.

"Looks like we're on the wrong road."

The Indian nodded agreement. They were. But they hadn't asked his advice when they made the wrong turn, so he hadn't given it. There is nothing superfluous about the Navaho. But by that time the disgruntled visitors were not interested in anthropology. They were disgusted with the whole country, and Sallie knew how they felt.

She was trying one of those oven-cooked meals which the cookbook recommended for large-scale feeding under circumstances as much like hers as she could find listed in its slick-paper pages. It came under the heading "Golf Dinner," and according to the cookbook there was nothing to it. Its preparation was simple, and then all you did was put it in the oven and close the door. There lay the hitch. The door of the wood stove she had inherited from Mr. Parquette would not close. She finally got it pounded shut, and the oven-cooked meal started to burn. She pried it open again and left it slightly ajar, and nothing cooked.

Their first importations, then, to Wide Ruins, were Butane Gas and the installation of an electric power plant—toward the modernizing of the kitchen. But here again they ran into trouble with the Indians.

In digging the pipelines through the yard the workers came upon some old stone mortars: odd fragments of ancient pottery of dull red and tan, scored with spiral designs. There was one whole jar filled with tiny colored shell beads. These last the Lippincotts learned later probably had been brought up from the Gulf by the first Indians to come upon the place. But the first they knew of the general excavation was the sight of Joe leaving work and heading for his wagon, with two of the stone mortars clutched tenderly to his bosom. He was on his way to Chambers to sell his loot Down by the Railroad, as he called the white civilization which met their own there at the edge of the reservation.

The whole astonishing racial strength of the Navahos has been built on the simple theory that when they saw something they wanted, it was their right to take it. That was all very interesting as a racial trait, but as a personal characteristic they

were going to have to live with, the Lippincotts felt it should
be curbed. They cornered Joe and asked him where he'd found
the mortars. Joe told them he'd found them up by his hogan.
They asked him three times, and each time he said the same
thing. They asked him a fourth time, and Joe, beginning to
shift and shuffle under the combination of the third degree
and the uncomfortable discovery that the young white people
should know to ask him four times, admitted that he had
found the mortars in their house yard.

That was one of the things they had learned at Canyon de
Chelley—that an Indian will lie three times, but if asked a
fourth, he will tell the truth, because if he doesn't, his lie will
come at him from all four sides, from the east and west and
north and south, and trap him.

"Bad Joe Toddy to steal!" They cudgeled him with frowns.

With his horizons thus closing in on him, the perspiration
started on Joe's leathery forehead, and he couldn't remember
what English he did know.

"Me good Indian!" he pleaded. "Me pick things oop, put
'em back—pick 'em oop, put 'em back!"

And he did. After that he never found a pretty pebble but
what he brought it to them. He was a nuisance about it. Jimmy
brought them pretty findings from the earth, too, but for a
different reason. From the pipeline excavation they found on
the table a handful of blue beads. The tiny cylindrical things
were showing up everywhere in the digging, of all colors, but
he had sorted out ones of a strange blue. They were like blue
fire in the palm.

But the other Indians were refusing to touch the stuff. It
was a superstitious fear, however, and not a moral one which
was holding them back. Indeed they refused to dig another
inch. Those relics they were disturbing belonged to the Old
Ones. Had they been relics of the Navaho dead which the

workmen had come upon, they would have fled the place and never come near it again. The horror of their dead, and anything having to do with their dead, is their uppermost Chindee—their chief taboo. These were not Navaho dead, however—they belonged to the Pueblo Old Ones, whose land this originally had been.

Probably in the first place when Broad House was put up by those ancient Pueblos, fertile fields had surrounded it. The Navahos never have bothered about raising crops themselves. They have always preferred wandering aristocratically around the country on their horses, herding sheep, and leaving the farming to their neighbors, the Pueblos. Then, in season, they would clean up on the Pueblo fields. The Pueblos would work and slave all year, and just at the peak of the harvest—zist!—along would come the Navahos and steal it. The Pueblos still call them the Naughty Navahos. And evidently after they'd taken their needs from the fields here at Kintiel, the fields themselves took their eye, so they acquired those too. At least it was Navaho country now, and not Pueblo. The Navahos have little respect for the Pueblos above ground, but just the same they weren't taking any chances with those underneath.

So Bill had to throw out all his carefully calculated pipelines and reroute the whole ditch system, making detours around the Old Ones. It was a gesture which was rewarded by a formal call from the medicine man.

The medicine man in that district was, they came to realize increasingly, one of the most respected ones on the reservation. And they themselves liked him immediately. They did not know what his real name was, but he was called Loukaichukai, because he was from the Loukaichukai Mountains. He came into the yard one day with all the dignity of a procession—a very old man in a sheepskin coat pinned together with safety pins, and with a handsome string of rough-cut turquoise hanging down over the pins. His thin old legs were wrapped with army leggings—left over from the days when he had taken the Big Walk into New Mexico with Kit Carson. His long gray hair was bundled low at the back of his neck. Under the shadow of his sombrero was a powerful face, with the years lined deeply in it and their wisdom mellowed in his eyes. There was a faint sardonic humor in those eyes, too. Most of all he was distinguished by that hauteur which is the chief characteristic of the best of his race. This pride in their race, which the first of them had put into it for themselves and their seed, had not gone away in Loukaichukai.

The Lippincotts shook hands with their caller—Indians like to shake hands. It makes them feel good. There was no word exchanged among them, and Sallie and old Loukaichukai sat down on the woodpile. Bill offered the medicine man a cigarette—careful to offer it upright, not directly. That was another important first thing they had learned—never to make any gesture which seemed to point at an Indian; it antagonized him. Also they had learned not to offer an Indian a cigarette out of the pack. That was because if they did, the Indian would take the whole pack.

Loukaichukai accepted the cigarette and a packet of paper matches Bill offered him. Then he had quite a time. He could see the flat little matches through the exposed side of the packet, and tried to get at them from that opening. Bill took the packet back, opened up the flap, drew a match and lit the cigarette for him. All this in a continuing silence. Loukaichukai could not speak English, and although Sallie and Bill were beginning to learn a little Navaho, there was something about the old man's dignity which kept them from experimenting with it on him. Besides, Navahos have little regard for talkative people. They consider the frugal use of words a virtue.

However, it was a silence strangely without strain, and old Loukaichukai smoked his cigarette with all the ceremonial measure of a peace pipe, and when it was done, he arose, and still with that assurance which seemed to have its roots in historic time, departed. They felt they had made a friend.

It was also during the rebuilding of the house that they received their first social invitation. It was from the carpenter who was doing the woodworking in the addition of a guest room and servant quarters—for that they had imported white labor from off the reservation. The carpenter was a friendly fellow and, just before he was through, invited them to a dance one night at his place. He lived a hundred miles away, on the other side of Gallup, but in that country distances mean nothing. It was always the first eighteen miles to Chambers which were the hardest.

But even so, they got to the dance early enough for Bill to help the ranch hands and bean growers, who were gathering for the party, lift the stove from the middle of the room and put it outdoors. Then, while the men stayed outside around the liquor keg that was out there too, Sallie tried to get acquainted with the women. All the women were sitting in chairs around the wall, stiff and silent, and staring straight in front of them. She began talking to the one beside her, but it seemed to make the other so unhappy, she gave it up. Since there seemed no point in burning herself out scintillating, she too sat and stared.

The orchestra came and went. Whenever anyone with a fiddle or mouth harp or guitar felt the urge, he came inside and struck up a tune. Then one by one each of the men would stamp in from the outside, stand in the doorway, run the women over with his eye until he found one that attracted him. That lucky one got summoned by a jerk backward of his head. She would get up, and go to him. They'd take hands, crook elbows, get set, lift a knee and gallop off determinedly. When the dance was over, the couple would stop abruptly right where they were, and the man would walk off and leave the lady standing. Nobody frittered away any time in light conversation while he danced.

Bill, finally feeling he was onto the etiquette of the affair enough to take a try at it, stood in the doorway, picked out a partner with his eye, summoned her with a jerk backward of his head, danced with her silently for ten minutes and left her duly in the middle of the floor. Then he found out she was from Columbia University, in the Southwest working on her doctor's degree.

It was spring before the house was really ready to begin living in. Their first spring in the desert. In other parts of the country it was April, which always brings the breath of new life with it. But here April had been just a hangover from winter. The winter, though, had not been so bad, once they got prepared for it. Indeed the days had been beautiful, with the snow staying crisp and in separate crystals like all the stars left over, and the sky that ran back of the hills as blue as Jimmy's fire-blue beads. Then in March that intensity had dulled. The snow had gone except for strips in the shadowed places, but no life showed yet. By April the desert earth was cracking with winter breaking up.

But it was not until late May, after the winter had gone and the sandstorms which followed were over, that spring began to look real—on the brown hills all around, and in the glisten to the deep green of the pinion needles. The sage made no sign. Sage never changes—it's always the same. But the cottonwoods began coming into leaf, and there were strikes of sun. Spring was real on the near hills, but the far ones—smooth rolls of slate and gray, even, tranquil—they seemed only dreams of it yet.

But days around the trading post had a bright sun to them, they had a warming earth, although fires still were needed in the house at night. Joe was going up into the mountains, where the pinions grew larger, for the big logs for the great stone fireplace at one side of the living room. Its hearth could take logs cut generously and stacked upright against the back of it, western fashion. Joe kept a pile of these logs stacked at one side of the hearth—gray twisted things that looked old and done for, but when they burned life was in them, and their sweetness stayed faintly in the air a long time afterward. But it took juniper chips to start them, so Joe kept a small pile of the crumbly yellow juniper kindling beside the gray pinion. At the other side of the wide hearth was the stone mortar of the Old Ones he had tried to take Down by the Railroad. Now it held big, blue-tipped matches. The other mortar he had started off with so confidently was shallower. It was more a pallet for grinding mineral coloring, and now it too was used for matches, on the mantel of the corner fireplace in the guest room, beside the books. Firelight gleamed off the copper conical fireplace in the library, and found a reflection of itself in the old round copper woodbox.

But there was no longer the cedary lift of wood burning in the kitchen stove. The kitchen was white porcelain and chrome, and had Sallie's old cook from home established in it, in a calm white apron. The calm had come with persuasion, however. Until the cook had landed in Wide Ruins she never had seen an Indian, except the ones in front of cigar stores and in wax in museums. And her introduction to a live one almost sent her back where she came from.

The first night she was there, Crip Chee paid a call. Crip Chee looked like a satyr, with one malformed hand like a cloven hoof. He was an Indian with a bad name, although in his lighter moments the Lippincotts had come to find that the love of a joke could go with his bad name, too. Crip Chee strode into the kitchen, through the laundry, up the back stairs, and into the cook's room. With his cloven hand crooked, a leer on his face, great earrings and all sorts of barbaric adornment to his costume which was barbaric enough anyway, Crip Chee appeared like a purposeful satyr. For a second Mrs. Sheets stood literally frozen. But Crip Chee, looking neither to right nor left, strode straight past her across the room and into her clothes closet, and shut himself in. Mrs. Sheets let out a blood-curdling yell and made it downstairs in one jump. They got Crip Chee routed out of her clothes closet, but it took them some time to convince her that Crip Chee's idea of humor was inclined to take a practical turn. Gradually Mrs. Sheets grew to like Wide Ruins, but she never liked Crip Chee.

The old stone house, which had struck them with its solidity the first time they saw it, was taking on life. It was a stone house that had been there a long time, and with the look and feel to it that it would last forever. Though originally it had been called Broad House, it was not so big for today as to make any claim to the pretentious possessiveness that a bigger stone house might—that might even strike one as a futile mocking gesture, as though elaborate lengths had been gone to to prove the briefness and instability of everything. It was only a small stone house, but it looked like some place to come to when it was needed and wanted—and some place that had been come to because the heart had come there unthinkingly first.

Jimmy was leaving his shy presents, not on the kitchen table any more, but on a table by the front door. They never caught him at it; they never knew when he left them. But they would find them. Once it was a picture of a mauve and pink mouse with gentle eyes, sitting in the curve of its pink tail, with a few well chosen live-green blobs of something growing around it as background. On the back of a piece of white stationery from the club car of the Chief, he did a bright-eyed little squirrel, with its light-touched stock of nuts and leaves around it an integral part of the picture. The small details of Jimmy's pictures were coming to be more and more an important part of them.

CHAPTER

4

THERE was the full smell of sage and pine in the air. The wind in the cottonwoods was lifting easy and fresh. It was early summer and every desert morning was like a new beginning—as though to say, "Look at the day's bright sun! Look at the day's good world!"—as though discovering it all over again. And when dark came, that was a natural thing, too. It came easily, rightly—the right end of a quiet day. There was a quiet goodness to all of it that first beginning of summer at Wide Ruins, and all of it different, and all belonging to the earth's good.

"Somebody took a lot of trouble about making this world—all the little things," marveled Sallie one evening. She was discovering the single white striping on every leaf of a vine that was beginning to twine up over the porch post.

Bill looked at the vine without too much interest. "Somebody slipped up on a few things, though. Look at corn borers. Most things people used to hate or were afraid of someone has found some use for. But I never heard anybody give a damn thing to a corn borer."

The store was being eaten through by them.

"I heard on the radio the other day an advertisement for an insecticide with a nitroglycerine base, called WHAM!" suggested Sallie. They had tried everything else, so they decided to try that, and sent for it.

During the months when they had been particularly occupied

37

making the house livable, they had hired a man to run the store for them who used to clerk for Cozy McSparron, over at Canyon de Chelley. Like Cozy, he had been born on the reservation and knew Indian trading and could speak Navaho —which was important, since almost no one around the Wide Ruins trading post spoke English. The clerk was a tall, fair man, with a twinkle almost hidden back in his eyes, whose name was Bill Cousins. Clan relationship being the broad and airy thing it is among the Navahos, he at once became known as Bill's Cousin among the customers.

The customers had been few at first, for there had been little to sell them. The original equipment with which the Lippincotts became Indian traders consisted mostly of dozens of beaver caps with ear tabs and the beaver eaten off, a few cans of tomatoes, flour drilled through by the corn borers, a supply of kerosene, a huge wooden mantel clock, and some odds and ends of personal clothing which included a silk tie and handkerchief set which Mr. Parquette had thrown into the bargain. Someone had sent it to him once for Christmas, but since he never used a tie or likely a handkerchief, it still was in its original box collecting dust, and became part of the Lippincotts' stock.

Although for the most part they left the running of the store to Bill Cousins those first months, they did a little with the business when they could, and their first real venture into Indian trading was the holding of a sale. They loaded one counter with all the leftover stock that was not too impossible, and on the other counter they laid out prizes—toy whistles, scraps of leather, cork-tipped cigarettes, some glassware of their own—things Indians would like to have but wouldn't buy. Also there were a lot of colored balloons which they'd brought back from a party at the Broadmoor Hotel in Colorado Springs. Every time a purchase was made from the sale counter, the purchaser was allowed to choose a prize.

It worked beautifully, and everyone had a fine time. John Galeno came early and stood all day long in front of the mantel clock which Bill had wound and set. He couldn't tell time, he just stood watching the little hands go around. Finally, at the very end of the day, he traded both the coyote pelt and the bobcat skin he'd brought along as spending money for it. Then he went out with the big wooden clock clutched tightly under his arm, home to the pile of brush where he lived at the edge of the canyon brim. Every morning thereafter as long as the Lippincotts were there, John Galeno would come trudging into the trading post with the clock tucked under his arm, to set its hands by Bill's watch. John Galeno wasn't going any place—except to sand paintings. John sat next to the medicine man and led the chants at sand paintings. John wasn't going any place, and he wasn't in any hurry. Still, the idea of time going around and around, doing the same thing over and over again, fascinated him and kept him puzzled.

Of all the prizes the toy balloons were the most sought after. Mrs. Beaver was so much taken by a yellow one that her husband finally bought a suit of long underwear so she could have it. Joe Toddy saw a big red one which so struck him that he bought a pair of gray striped morning trousers—which he subsequently wore only on state occasions, turned up several times at the cuffs since they were too long. But it was the red balloon which really intrigued him. He took it outside and sat down on a log against the store and blew a little red bubble that got bigger and bigger, with his pleasure in the feat going right up with it. But as usual, Joe went to extremes. He puffed out his cheeks once too often. Then he sat bewil-

dered and disappointed. He couldn't understand it. A minute
ago it had been such a pretty bubble, and now all he had was
just a little damp rag in his hand.

It had been a fine day and nobody wanted to go home. One
of the Lippincotts' predecessors at the post—the woman of the
jeans and pistols—had shut up shop at the end of the day by
driving the Indians out with her guns. And Bill himself
learned that day to begin closing the store thereafter at four, so
he really could shut the door by six.

It had been a colorful day. Horses had been tethered, their
heads patiently hanging, out in the yard and over by the
sheep-corral fence across the road. The sheep-corral fence was
made of juniper posts set upright and close together, with no
thought for uniformity or size, and made a jagged line against
the hill behind it. There were old heavy-wheeled wagons with
red water barrels in them. One of these wagons was hitched
to a black team and had a white horse tethered at right angles
to it. On the ground beside the wagons, during the noon hour,
sat groups of Indian women in their red and yellow and blue
full calico skirts and with their dark velvet blouses brightened
by silver buttons, eating the lunches of dark bread they'd
brought with them. Their black hair was bound low on their
necks, like raven's wings outspread, and held by soft bands of
white wool thread. The levis of the men were topped with
brilliant shirts, with their lean waists weighed down by heavy
silver concha belts, and their inky hair held back from their
Mongoloid faces by bright silk headbands. That day Joe Toddy
wore his musty red headband rakishly tied in a bow over his
right ear. The Navaho men who came to the sale studied the
new young white trader with level regard, and the women kept
peeking at Sallie over their shawls, not wanting the white
woman to see them looking.

There was the low flow of Navaho—a guttural language

but so softly spoken it sounded like quiet water flowing through a gravel bed. The Navaho language has stayed remarkably pure and close to its Athapascan origin, in spite of all battering from the outside. It is a grammatically complicated language, but Bill was trying to learn it—as a matter of good business, since it was the language of his customers. And Sallie had a lesson in it that day. Sallie recognized, as he was leaving the sale with Mr. Parquette's silk tie and handkerchief set, a young Navaho named Paul who was helping them build their swimming pool. (That Wide Ruins had ever been touched at all was an archeological disaster. But since a trader before them, in 1900, already had thoroughly desecrated the ruins by converting them into a store and a house, the Lippincotts felt they might as well finish the job. So they were converting what had probably been one of the ancient terraces, into a badminton court, and were making a swimming pool out of one of the lower excavations where Indians about the time of the earliest Spanish invasion had been wont to closet themselves for their ceremonial rituals.) Sallie knew the young mason spoke English, and as he passed she said, "Hello, Paul."

He grinned and said, "Hello," and started on. Then he thought better of it, stopped, turned around and came back.

"Ya ta hey," he corrected, in Navaho.

"Ya ta hey," repeated Sallie.

Not quite satisfied with her pronunciation he said it for her again, and Sallie dutifully repeated it. But since that didn't quite suit him either, they went through the performance a third time, and then a fourth. At the fourth try he listened critically, said "O," which is the Navaho equivalent for Okay, turned on his heel and left.

It had been a colorful day with a sense of give and take about it, and the end of it was something to see. Men and women of the proud, dominant race, who still persisted in the

ways of their kind and dealt only surfacely in the doings of
the white people, were going off up the hills from the trading-
post yard, or up the road in their wagons or on their horses—
the ones on horses singing the Navaho riding song—with toy
balloons floating gayly out behind them.

From its very beginning Indian trading in the Southwest
has been a picturesque business. And in the old days there
used to be a fortune in it. That was when there were only a
handful of traders in all the twenty-odd thousands of square
miles of Navaho reservation.

The original grant of one of these early traders, whose post
was not far from the one at Wide Ruins, had run clear from
the Rio Grande to Rio Puerco. He had died some years before,
but Sallie and Bill heard a good deal about him still. He had
been Spanish, but looked like Theodore Roosevelt, except that
his fierce white mustaches had turned up instead of down. He
had once gone hunting in Africa with Roosevelt, and the old
Moorish-type house in the desert had its walls so covered with
trophies from that trip, and with Spanish ancestral things
which had come around the Horn, the walls themselves were
completely hidden. He had been quite a figure in the Southwest, that trader, and sometimes the new young traders would
go call on his daughters. The daughters would sit primly in
high old rockers, working black lace Spanish handkerchiefs
while they made polite conversation about how hard clothes
were to get in that part of the country, and about the servants
—and a Navaho maid would serve formal tea.

Another of their neighbors from the old days was a sandy-
haired Scotchman who never had tanned, although he had
been in that country fifty years. He still had a burr to his
tongue, and in his time had been a very independent trader.
He had charged twice as much for his flour as everyone else—
and paid twice as much for the wool he took in. When every-

one else was paying ten cents a pound for wool, he paid twenty, and then would add up the transaction rapidly in his mind, so that the Indians never quite knew just how they stood with him. He never put any price marks on the store items, and he never tried to buy anything. He would name his price, and if the Indian didn't take it, the Scotchman would shrug, go over to a pile of pawned saddles, sit down, and roll himself a cigarette. He could afford to wait.

He would have had things pretty much his own way out there, had it not been for a lifelong feud he carried on with his nearest competitor. One time the latter put coffee down to a price far below cost. When the Scotchman got wind of that shady deal, he made some comments along the general line of thought that that crooked so-and-so wouldn't know the meaning of the word honest even when rivers began running crosswise. Whereupon he took a blowtorch, and carefully singed a dozen bags of coffee from off his own shelf. To the next Indian who came in complaining that they'd heard coffee at the next post was only such a price, he said scornfully, "You mean that stuff from the fire sale in Gallup? I've got some of that, too. It isn't any good. Here, I'll just give you a pound—" and he handed the befuddled customer a bag of the singed coffee.

That had been in the days when it took sometimes two weeks to get to Gallup in a spring wagon, and when the nearest of trading posts had fifty miles between them. Now there was a trading post every fifteen miles or so, traders were under a $50,000 government bond, and the trading business was supposed to be under government supervision—although in all the four years the Lippincotts had Wide Ruins, the post was visited only once by a government inspector, and that check-up was made at the Lippincotts' request. The inspector came and laid down a few general rules: that no liquor should be sold at the post, that there was to be no issuance of the tin coins which a good many of the old traders used to hand out, that honest weights and measures be used, and exorbitant prices not be charged.

There still is the story, however, of one of the present-day traders at Gallup who sold an itinerant Indian a pair of sunglasses. The Indian came into the shadowy store blinking from the brilliant noonday outside and got sold a pair of black sunglasses. After the usual dallying of an hour or so, and the usual bottle of pop had been indulged in, the Indian started home. Almost at once he was back, looking forlorn. He told the trader he hadn't realized it was so late—it was getting dark outside, and he was a long way from home, in a strange country. Whereupon the trader said a few well chosen words of comfort—and sold him a lantern and a quart of kerosene.

There is some justification for this general practice of shenanigan among traders by small means and great, and for their scales usually being off, because their customers have their little ways themselves. All wool which comes in to the trader has some sand in it, but sometimes a Navaho can manage to get as much as ten or fifteen pounds in one wool sack. Sand is harder to detect in wool than rocks, although frequently rocks are softly embedded in it too. And when an Indian brings in lambs to the post, he is sure to have watered them until they weigh three or four pounds more than they should.

Sallie and Bill, however, set out to combat this mistrust on both sides in what tangible ways they could think of, such as teaching the sheep sellers to read the scales for themselves when they brought their lambs to be sold. Then duplicate copies of the sale were made, so that the Navaho could have a record of the transaction also. Word began getting around that the new young white traders seemed likely to deal fairly.

Also, the new young traders had a respect for the people

they had come to deal with. It was a respect which Kit Carson himself—the only white man who ever understood them well enough to conquer them—impressed upon General Carleton, who had commissioned him to rid the country of them. And in his turn, after this swift, strong tribe had finally been captured and taken to New Mexico—and then returned to their own lands again by the government itself—General Carleton wrote to Washington a long letter in their behalf. In part the letter reads:

Unless you make in the law all arrangements here contemplated, you will find this interesting and intelligent race of Indians will fast diminish in numbers, until within a few years only not one of those who boasted the proud name of Navaho will be left to upbraid us for having taken their birthright and then left them to perish. With other tribes whose lands we have acquired, ever since the Pilgrims stepped on shore at Plymouth, this has been done too often. For pity's sake, if not moved by any other consideration, let us, as a great nation, for once treat the Indian as he deserves to be treated. It is due to ourselves as well as to them that this be done.

As a matter of actual fact, this "interesting and intelligent race" evidently had no intention of perishing meekly. Far from diminishing in numbers, it has increased rapidly and steadily—the only race of Indians in the country which has. And through it all they have stayed close to their way of thought, which, like their speech, has stayed remarkably unscathed despite the tremendous changes it has been subjected to. It had its origins in legendary beginnings so intricate and so complicated that the more the Lippincotts came to know of it, the more they realized that neither they nor any other white person would ever be able to comprehend it fully. The everyday lives of the people they had come to deal with were ruled by ancient small details which never would occur to the white mind. But the young traders tried.

They learned never to point, and which way to spin a basket. This latter Sallie discovered when she was examining an antique basket which had been brought in to be pawned. She was twirling it idly on the counter as she looked at the patterns in it. Joe Toddy happened to amble into the store just then, stopped short, and turned pale. He made a leap toward her and said "Stop!" in such a thoroughly frightened tone of voice that Sallie leaped as far in the other direction. Joe told her she'd bring all the Chindee in the world down on their heads by twirling a basket in that direction! And then he hastily twirled it the right way, to show her.

Also they learned never to ask an Indian his name directly, nor to further commit that breach of etiquette by trying to find it out from anyone else directly, either. Still, names would be a great help in the system of bookkeeping Bill was trying to set up. The bookkeeping at the Wide Ruins store when they had taken it over had consisted of chalk marks all over the dark adobe walls—four vertical ones, with the fifth one crossing them off, like a game score. Perhaps Mr. Parquette knew which was what, but nobody else did.

One day, early in their experience as traders, a man came into the store and asked for enough credit to buy ten bales of hay. Naturally Bill wanted to be careful to whom he gave credit, if the store was to make any money, so he asked the man who he was. But at what seemed a very normal question, asking a credit customer's name, the customer bridled and stalked coldly and furiously out of the store. He stood outside with his arms crossed, glaring. After a couple of hours he came back in again, and again asked for credit. Again Bill asked what his name was. At that, the Indian began pacing up and down like a mad bull, throwing his arms around and muttering angrily, "What does he want to know my name for? What is he going to do with it? What right has he to it?"

Finally Bill Cousins told Bill—in Navaho, loud enough for the Indian to hear—that the man's name was Mouse's Son.

At that the Indian wheeled, slammed over to the counter and banged his fist down at the indignity of a name like that being his.

"That is not my name! My name is Soshei Begai!"

Then, realizing he had been tricked into revealing it, he stormed out of the store and went home and changed his name and the name of his whole family—and that they never did find out. In the end, they settled for nicknames.

Throughout this whole venturing first year, Bill Cousins was a great help to them. Typical of the white people born and raised on the reservation, he had no philosophical interest in the Indians, or curiosity about their way of life. But he knew about trading with them, and what was of real importance, he knew how to joke with them. The Navaho humor is a great part of them, but it comes quickly, unobtrusively—they are wary of any heavy quipping which demands response. Fortunately for Sallie and Bill, this was one angle of the business they could fall in with without trying.

It was an especially lucky happenstance the day Crip Chee came into the store to look over the newcomers. This was before his visit to the cook, and before they knew about his rightfully earned record for rape, larceny, bootlegging bad liquor, and almost any of the other vices. Also he had a habit of periodically descending on the Wide Ruins trading post and shooting it up.

The Navahos are a live-and-let-live people. They will take a good deal from their kind until suddenly, when it comes to a point which no longer can be tolerated, they turn and put an end to it. But their reaction to Crip Chee was not so free or neat. Because of his cloven hoof for a hand, and his whole satyrical cast, they were afraid of him, even as they despised him for it. They avoided him when they could, and when they couldn't, they tormented him.

All this Sallie and Bill found out about him later. That first day they merely saw an Indian with a leer on his face, his ear lobes weighed down by great blobs of turquoise, his whole ragged person barbarically adorned, and with one misshapen hand. He looked the perfect wicked pirate. And after his first start, Bill regarded him interestedly and said, in English, "Why you old devil—I know a man named Robert Louis Stevenson who would have loved knowing you."

The Indian looked at the young white man in surprise. Crip Chee could not understand English, but he could understand the twinkle in the white man's eyes. And slowly Crip Chee's eyes began to crinkle at their own corners.

"Huh!" he said. With that the ruffian swaggered over to the candy counter, very recklessly bought a lollipop, took it outside and leaned against the store wall and bashfully ate it.

It was such a ludicrous picture that Sallie ran for the camera. The more unsophisticated Navahos are afraid of having their picture taken, because they think something of themselves is being taken from them. They pose for a picture only with the understanding that a copy of it will be given back to them, so that what was taken away will be returned. But those who have been around have learned to be more worldly about it. And when Sallie reappeared with the camera, Crip Chee set himself to pose, paused, and warned in Navaho which Bill Cousins interpreted for her, "I charge a quarter to have my picture taken."

"That's funny," relayed Sallie back to him, "because that's just what I charge to take a picture."

"Huh!" chortled Crip Chee. "Huh, huh. Huh!"

Crip Chee did not mend his ways in general, but so far as the store was concerned he never did anything more dastardly after that than could have come under the heading of practical joking. Sallie and Bill wondered a little—wondered at least if perhaps those other times, when he had come to the store and shot his way out, had also started as a joke. With perhaps back of the joke a realization of how unlike and alone he was by worldly measure, and yet sometimes with such a need of people that he would approach them, only to have them turn from him in loathing and fear, and hurt him. And when he was spurned, that evil in him—there was no getting round its existence—came out in revenge. The leer on his face had come from a knife slash, so he knew the physical anguish of revenge as well as mental. And his jokes had turned mean.

Because of the condition of the roads there were few casual comers to the trading post that first winter and early spring. But by late May the roads were fairly passable, and one day two tourists stopped in. They were of the variety most apt to lay themselves open to the cut of Navaho sarcasm. A few days before another party of travelers had happened upon the place and looked about the store curiously, and at the Indians in it. They had committed no more breach, however, than to make those general remarks everyone reads at some time or other about a primitive race.

"They are just like children, aren't they?" whispered one woman in the party to Sallie.

Sallie laughed a little, because just a few minutes before she had overheard an Indian woman lean over and in an interested undertone say to another—at seeing the tourists so eagerly examining everything in the old store—"They act like children."

The second couple did not get off so easily. They arrived at the store during one of its lulls. There are frequent apparent lulls in the trading-post business, when the trader seems to have nothing more to do than sit half the day on a counter, while an Indian woman with a flour sack of wool on her lap sits on the floor in a corner as though she were waiting the end of time, and an Indian man stands indifferently staring at nothing. Actually the woman with the sack is making up her mind whether sensibly to take calico in exchange for her wool, or have a little fun as she goes along and buy herself a pair of silk stockings. And the trader is waiting for the man in the doorway to come nearer his price on the hundred head of sheep the man has come to sell.

On this day when the tourists came in, everything was quiet. A few minutes before there had been laughter. Joe Toddy had been dusting. Every night the place got thoroughly lysoled, but at the moment Joe was merely dusting off the leather goods with a big oily rag. He dusted around the store to the line-up of Indians sitting silent and motionless on a bench, and without any change in expression he went right on down the line and dusted them off, too. Everybody thought that was very funny. But now the laughter had quieted again.

Old Loukaichukai, the medicine man, was standing mildly in front of the cold stove. Jimmy was behind the stove, by the woodbox—as usual keeping back out of the way but looking and listening. At the white people's entrance, Loukaichukai sent them a casual, uncritical regard, which sharpened with his second survey.

While the woman flicked through a lot of things in the store she didn't believe she wanted, her husband proceeded to tell Bill about the trading-post business, in an authoritative tone of voice. He'd been on a dude ranch once and knew about the West. Bill leaned back against the cash register and listened. Since the other knew, there was no need for him to say anything.

Then the couple discovered Loukaichukai. They went up

close to the old Indian and stared at him as though he were an animal in a zoo, and made audible comments and asked questions about him. The old medicine man could not understand what they were saying, but there was no mistaking the thinness of perception in their tones and expressions—although he did not appear to see them. The man who could remember when there had been power and might in his people's hand, looked just past them. He did not appear to hear them or see them. He did not seem to know they were there. Gradually they got an odd look on their faces as though maybe they *weren't* there. Their comments dwindled, and as soon as they could, they left.

When the tourists had gone, Bill complimented old Loukaichukai on the poise with which he had met the situation. Loukaichukai brought his gaze back from the distance with which he somehow had managed to surround himself so the intruders could not get across it. He regarded the younger man with the mild satisfaction of an old eagle who has not yet perished for lack of prey.

"My son," he said, "you have learned to ignore by your manner the people who annoy you. You should learn to ignore them with your mind. Then nothing they say or do can hurt you, because for you they do not exist."

The Navahos as a race bear no blanket respect for the whites, merely because they are white. They tolerate them, and if they once give their friendship it is the genuine thing. But let them detect any note of condescension, and their attitude wipes the whole white race off the face of the earth.

At some time during all this, when nobody had noticed, Jimmy had gone back to his drawing table in the ware room. That afternoon he painted porcupines. He painted several pages of porcupines, one right after another. That was the way he worked. With the heels of his yellow shoes hooked over

a high rung of his chair, the little boy would sit at his drawing
table for hours, his dark head bent intently, working steadily.
When one picture was done, he would lay the paper to one side,
and without even raising his head to look up, would reach for
another paper and start in on it. He did not leave it for a while
and do something else, as most children did. He kept at it
until it was done. And when it was done he would go play
marbles, or ride his pony, or get in a fight, or—a little incon-
gruously—make himself a set of bow and arrows and a feather
headband and play Indian. But while he painted, he painted.
And he took streaks of painting the same thing in different
ways.

His porcupine pictures started out with one porcupine standing precariously on a row of grass blades that looked like a
rake. In the next picture there were two porcupines, bigger
and black, with great yellow spines ruffled up like plumes and
with the eyes of little minds set far back in their heads. They
were flanking a pine tree set squarely in the middle of the
page, with the pine tree not so much a likeness as something
that might have been laid out with a ruler. One porcupine
had a paw on the pine trunk, while on the other side its com-
panion was examining the earth as though he doubted it.

In the last set two fat porcupines with hanging jowls were
pussyfooting their way across the page with an expression of
pleased wisdom on their fools' faces.

Sallie never tried to direct or change the pictures that Jimmy
painted, but when she walked in later and saw this lot, she
decided any more like them would begin keeping her awake
nights. So she put up a sign of protest. On a piece of cardboard
she printed in big slashing letters, NO MORE PORCUPINES! The
next night the sign was still there, and down at the very bottom,
in the righthand corner, in the smallest possible letters, like a

whispered echo, was *"no more porcupines."* That day, instead, the little boy painted three stuffily startled green goats.

Indian trading, even in 1939, was still a colorful business, and an unpredictable one. Even with their apprenticeship at Canyon de Chelley and the help of Bill Cousins, it had been mainly a matter of going ahead themselves and taking a chance, and growing into it gradually. And although there was no longer a fortune in the business, by dint of keeping books— being careful to whom they gave credit, watching the outside markets, and going along with the Navahos in what ways they could—the store was beginning to make money. By the time their first early summer in the business came around, they felt they were about ready to square away and really go into it. The house was done, and they could turn their attention more fully to developing the business end of the venture. The most they had learned that first year, of course, was that Indian trad- ing was not a business they could step into and revolutionize overnight. Its roots went too deep and too wide for that. But they hoped to modernize at least the physical aspects of it.

This they had done nothing about yet, except paint the inside of the store. But even under the paint, the counters stayed the heavy old-fashioned wooden ones which cut in at the bottom. The floor was still flagstone and dirt, and the corn borers had such a hold on the place from the years that nothing they had yet tried had successfully exterminated them. Toward this, of course, they were sending for the insecticide Sallie had heard advertised over the air.

It came just before they left for a trip to California. While they were in San Francisco they went to the World's Fair, where Bill had been asked to give a radio talk on life in a Navaho trading post. Just as he was finishing the talk a tele- gram was handed him. It contained a last-minute flash on the subject. The store had blown up. WHAM, the insecticide with the nitroglycerine base, had done its work!

When they rushed back they found that Joe had decided, in one of those bursts of enthusiasms he got, that if a little WHAM was good, a lot of it would be better. He'd gotten rid of the corn borers, all right. They'd gone out through the roof, along with the rest of the inside of the store. But the roof had dropped back, and was on crooked—with all kinds of things sticking out from under it: rakes, hoes, wheelbarrows, shreds of clothing. Bill found his hat hanging to a splintered cornice, and put it on. The hat was all right, except for a hole burned in the back brim, and thus he came by the nickname Burned Hat.

Since they had been forced into it, they decided they might as well go the whole way and do the thing up right. By midsummer the Wide Ruins store had a cement floor and glass counters which could be hosed off twice a day with great ease. There were two new windows cut into the walls, and the stock on the new shelves were things they had learned the Indians consider of value. There was electric refrigeration and a water fountain. When they first had taken over the store, there had been a water pipe by the door with a tin cup chained to it, and all the Indians had drunk from the same cup. They had taken away the tin cup and put in paper cups. Then all the Indians had drunk from the same paper cup. They never did figure out a way to keep the Indians from putting their mouths down close over the bubbling fountain, delightedly.

But before they had a chance to try, they realized that although the new store now had everything to attract customers, they had no customers. This they could not understand, until Joe Toddy explained, hesitantly. The Indians were afraid to come back to it. They felt the store had blown up because the Anazazis, the Old Ones who used to live at Wide Ruins, were angry for some reason. He told them that the store was Chindee—taboo.

Here was a situation they did not know how to cope with, and they appealed to Loukaichukai. They asked if he knew how they could appease the Anazazis, and clear the atmosphere in general. The old medicine man replied gravely after a long time that there was a ceremony which could be held, and they complied.

With Loukaichukai leading, the three of them trouped into the store, Joe bringing up the rear, as interpreter. Old Loukaichukai shut the door. He spread out his blanket on the new cement floor back of the dry goods counter and asked Sallie and Bill to kneel. Then he gave them each a medicine bundle to hold—some pieces of petrified wood which had been polished to show the long-ago color of jasper locked in their years, and feathers with turquoise tied into them. While they held the charms, Loukaichukai sat down facing them and chanted— a wild chanting repeated the mystic four times. At the end of the chanting he sprinkled sacred corn pollen on their palms, instructing them to taste it, and then throw it upward to the gods.

With that they all arose, and made a solemn procession from the dry goods department out through the kitchen—since that would be the east toward which all Navaho ceremonies point. From the kitchen door they sallied out into the yard and up its eastern slope, and at the top they stood a while, while Loukaichukai sang a little song and went through some motions. They all sprinkled what they had left of the sacred corn pollen on a little pinion tree, and buried the feathers with the turquoise at its roots. Then they went back down into the trading-post yard, and Loukaichukai opened the door.

Despite its incongruities, it had been a very impressive ceremony. And at its end, as Sallie and Bill stood together thanking the old man, looking into his eyes and liking him for his sincerity and his dignity, he suddenly took them aback.

"Why did you ask me to do that?" he asked them. "You are white people, and white people do not believe in our gods."

Bill made a careful reply. "We believe all gods are the same. But we are strangers in your country, and do not know how to approach the gods in the Navaho way, that is why we asked you."

The old medicine man looked at them again, as long a time as when they had first made their request, and then there came a faint warming to his sharp old eyes, slowly, as though it were coming from far in. They did not give him money for the ceremony he had performed for them, as they would not have given money to a friend for some kindly service. But they gave him a present. They had brought back a box of seaweed candy from California, and when they gave it to him, they explained it had been made from flowers that grew under the sea.

The old man accepted it with interest. Then he asked them gravely if the next time they went to the sea, they would bring him back some white sand, and some black sand, and a wave.

CHAPTER

5

LITTLE WOMAN came into the store one morning with a Navaho rug rolled up under her velvet-bloused arm. The bundle was almost as big as she, Little Woman being just a shrivel of a woman and wrinkled as an old squash. But she gave Bill a snaggle-toothed beam as she shoved the rug across the counter at him.

"Present for you," she said, in Navaho.

"Well—" said Bill, pleased, and opened it up. Then he stood looking at it. It was a bordered rug of terrific yellow, with HELL woven into it in bitter black.

"Says 'Hello,'" grinned Little Woman.

Bill looked at it again, doubtfully. "Where's the O?"

"No room for the O," said Little Woman, unconcerned.

It became the Lippincotts' doormat, and one of their favorite possessions. Nevertheless they began to realize that the traffic in the famous Navaho rugs had fallen into sorry ways in the Wide Ruins community. This was deplorable, not only from the practical point of view, since most of the money in the trading business lies in the rug market, but also because the Navaho blanket is intrinsic in the whole proud history of Navaho survival.

A romantic survival, according to Charles Amsden, the Executive Secretary of the Southwest Museum, who says of it: "The romantic career of that handful of Athapascan people, who seemingly filtered through the mountain valleys of the southwest Rockies between 1000 and 1500 A.D., to become in an astonishingly short time the scourge of a far-flung line of stout Pueblo and Spanish communities—lords of territory comparable to New England, and the largest tribe of Indians in America. Warlike, this astonishing people defied the armed forces of the United States within the memory of living men—peaceful, it has sent the fame of its distinctive blankets to the ends of the earth. Between these meager factual details lies an epic human drama."

It is the drama of a strong people taking from other races whatever appeals to them and adapting it to their own. When the Spaniards came into their country, the Navahos let their Indian neighbors, the Pueblos, do the warring. They themselves kept aloof from the whole squabble. They merely swooped down and impartially raided both sides. They helped themselves liberally to the Spanish sheep, and since the Pueblo women— left home while their men went scalping—looked good to them, they had some of them, too. They took their needs arrogantly, by right of considering themselves The People.

Also the barbaric pulses of The People were quickened by the flaming red of the Spanish breeches as they watched the intruding soldiers go marching across their desert. So, without any to-do in the matter, they acquired the beautiful red Spanish pants. These they took home and gave to their women, who eagerly unraveled this European flannel known as bayeta, and rewove it into chief blankets and squaw skirts of their own designing, for which collectors and museums since have paid thousands of dollars.

It was the Pueblo captives who introduced to the Navahos the art of this weaving. But the captors soon were surpassing the captives in the stolen art. They wove with the long silky wool of the stolen Spanish Merino sheep, and with the flaming

European bayeta. Then they touched up their haul with some effort of their own. The women began going into the desert around them for roots and leaves and berries to concoct new colors. And this whole turn in their history, which wheeled it around weaving, was to direct the destiny of all Navahos to come.

The earliest known historical reference to Navaho weaving is in an excerpt from a letter from Governor Chacon in 1794: "They work their wool with more delicacy than the Spaniards. Men as well as women go decently clothed." Later, in 1799, Cortez mentions that "the manufacture of serge, blankets, and other coarse cloth more than suffice for the consumption of their own needs and they go into the province of New Mexico with the surplus." In 1812 Pino categorically places Navaho weaving at the head of the Southwest industries.

Because weaving had become a dominant factor in their tribal life, it was not the force of American arms which finally subdued that swift, wild race, but the canny denial to them of their sheep by Kit Carson. But later when the government realized its mistake in trying to incarcerate them in the military reservation at Fort Sumner in New Mexico, and returned them—a chastened and diminished, but still proud people—to their own lands which even today have changed little from their original boundaries, the government itself augmented their flocks to a working basis again.

Thus their tendency toward herding has stayed strong in them throughout their history. But the art of their weaving, which is equally as old, has fallen by the wayside—as Little Woman's rug made plainly clear. Perhaps it was an example of the extreme, but all over the country in lesser ways living rooms and dens were being outraged by the same bad weaving, the same thin machine-made yarn and cotton warp, the same hid-

eous colors from commercial dyes. And if the rugs didn't come
right out with that engaging frankness and spell hell, their
designs looked like it.

So, with Little Woman's present, Sallie and Bill set out to
revamp the rug business around Wide Ruins. They began it
by announcing that they would refuse to buy any rug which
came in with a border around it. The step was taken for two
reasons. The first was a sheerly personal one with Sallie. She
objected to rugs with borders. They always made her feel
as though she should walk around them, or else skip over them.

The other reason for reverting to the borderless rug was to
repurify the art. The border so familiarly associated with the
Navaho rug was not traditional, they found. The flashy rug of
isolated figures whose only tie was that they were held in by
the same border, was the product of a comparatively recent
commercial pressure. The best of the earliest of the old chief
blankets, they made sure from the survivals of them in the
museums of the Southwest, were of simple horizontal stripes—
and of colors that seem of the earth itself.

As was only natural in work wrought by people of the
earth, whose cadence was set by sun and sky and mountains and
growing things, and whose days came and went by line in that
southwest country—here the strong line of the mountains, the
deep blue mountains, against a sun going down red; there a
lower horizon of long golden yellow, with the cactus standing
out brown; then the mountains again, their clean line inked
to black now by night coming and set against the very last of
the green-gray day till tomorrow. There was a rhythm and
flow to the old Navaho blankets, a sense of continuing that
belonged to that country.

So Sallie and Bill began the revitalizing by asking for simple
horizontal stripes. And they meant it. Disgruntled weavers
found themselves trudging back home again with a bordered

rug they'd brought to the store to trade for tomatoes or American Beauty silk shirts or as down payment on a wagon. If they wanted tomatoes and fancy shirts and a wagon, they'd have to begin leaving off the borders. They didn't like it, but they did it; there wasn't anything else they could do.

Consequently rugs with the old-time stripes began showing up, and the Lippincotts bought them according to promise. But they couldn't sell them, nor would they have been proud to if they could. The weavers still were using the cheap tourist-trade dyes. They were the only dyes the younger ones knew, and the dyes the older ones had come to prefer.

And why not? In the old days, if a woman wanted to throw a little mustard into her pattern, she had to hie herself out over trackless desert to hunt for miles in that country of sparse vegetation for enough canaigre root to make the ensuing process worth while: pounding it to powder between two stones, boiling and reboiling it, and finally setting it with the favorite mordant of urine carefully saved up in an earthen pot outside the hogan. With proper manipulating, if you knew your boiling time and the right combination of herbs, that mustard color could be richened to old gold, or yellow brown, or even to an olive green. For the pure clear yellow, the flowering tops of goldenrod were boiled with a little fried gum, or mixed with some saline rock which had been made into a paste. The making of those famous lasting colors in the old blankets took time and painstaking toil on the part of those early chemists.

But why stew around over a lot of greasewood fire boiling up your own dyes when you could climb in the wagon and ride to the trading post and buy a packet of powder already made up and that didn't even need any urine to set it? And why be afraid any more of that bane of perfection which used to cause the painstaking weaver to make some purposeful mistake somewhere, so that she might not bring down the curse of the gods

—in jealousy of so much beauty as she was humanly achieving? The new quick tourist trade wasn't looking for perfection. They wanted something big and bright to show for their money, and they wanted it in a hurry.

So why bother with the old slow carding of your own wool by hand, and sitting for hours in the summer sun spinning with distaff—spinning three and four times over till the yarn was satisfyingly fine—when you could take your raw sheep pelt to the store and trade it for yarn machine-spun, and dyed to boot? What if it did make a loose weave? The white man didn't care any more about the firm, old-type weaving than he did the old dignity of color, or the old tranquillity of design.

Hence in looking up the records of Navaho weavings, Sallie and Bill found the weavers had come into an easy heyday of commercial dyes and a dominating pattern guaranteed to stun the passing eye and do a land-office business for the shrewd early traders. The weavers themselves didn't do badly in that era of big-time production. Government figures show that in 1912 they were doing a half-million dollar business on that basis.

However, the rugs they were whisking out at that rate might have been stunning, but you can't stun people all day long, year in and year out, and there came a lull in the Navaho rug market due to the fact that people in homes all over the country were beginning to take an edgy look at their eager bargains of the Wild West, and decide that enough was enough and perhaps what the house needed now was something a little more quiet.

It was in such a slough-off that Little Woman brought in her rug, and the adventuring Lippincotts were finding that, deprived of the geometric flashy cover-up of big design, the bad weaving and glaring analine dyes now were too obvious to pass in any of the good markets.

In the original blankets the colors were deep and rich, yet soft as those of the earth itself. And those delicate, lasting colorants could come only of the things of the earth. So Sallie and Bill went about the revival of the use of the old vegetable dyes.

In the summer they had spent at Canyon de Chelley, one of the things that had interested them particularly had been the pioneering work that the trading post there was doing in the revival of the use of vegetable dyes. With that as a beginning, they went into further research of their own, as they went along teaching what they were learning to the young commercial weavers around Wide Ruins, and learning some things themselves, from the older ones who remembered. They learned of the wild privet root for a yellow-green; sage for a dulling of that color, and canaigre root for the yellow that verged on brown; black walnut for the actual brown; and red from the inner lining of juniper roots—with the juniper berries doing for the dull blue, and indigo for the deep. The almond came from mountain mahogany; tan, pink, and a gray from certain ground rocks and clay. Green with gray in it came from rock lichen, and the old deep black from pinion gum, with its depth secretly got from the red of the sumac.

Thus the colorings which began coming into the store were more pastel, and some interest in the Wide Ruins rugs commenced to filter out through the markets, and to bring occasional purchasers to the trading post itself.

One day two fliers on leave from a field in California stopped in. They came to the place knowing nothing about it except that it was a trading post called Wide Ruins which had some interesting rugs for sale. They saw the rugs, but incidentally. It was Saturday afternoon, and finding the store door closed, they tried the old stone house next door. Their knock was answered by a pert young Navaho maid whose uniform fitted smartly over her flat hips. Bess was the latest addition to the Lippincotts' household. Like that of their handy man, Bess's broken English dwelt on the r's and hissed the s's. Unlike Joe, however, whose English was apt to slur bewilderedly, every word Bess spoke kicked up its heels. But her harsh laughter was likable, and her black eyes very bright. As she opened the door to the rug buyers she arched her black brows inquiringly, stood swinging her arms independently, and slung at them, "Whatchoo want?"

Beginning to feel a little uncertain, they told her they'd like to look at some rugs.

"Hokay," said Bess, and ushered them into a long great fireplaced living room and deposited them on the window seat where they sat with their uncertainty increasing as various other signs of a life they hadn't expected to find in the middle of a desert began to crisscross their line of vision. Sallie and Bill were having guests that weekend, and the two rug buyers who had come to deal with Indian traders turned in surprise as a couple in shorts came in carrying badminton racquets. While they were beginning to wonder, another couple came in from riding. Startled, they turned at the shadow of guns falling on them from the window behind them. But it was only the target shooters coming back. Finally Sallie showed up, in a bathing suit. They trailed her in bewilderment as she dripped out into the rug room back of the store, looked confusedly at a lot of rugs, and stayed meekly to dinner. At dinner everybody decided to go to a square dance that was being held in the schoolhouse of a neighboring post and they all went sailing off in the truck over the awful road to Klagatoh—and even though the fliers flew a P-38, they'd been worried.

But by the time they had promenaded a few times around the primary room of the Klagatoh schoolhouse (the primary chairs having been pushed thoughtfully back against the wall), the

fliers were stamping out western rhythm from shoulder to boot
heel along with the rest of them.

> Swing your opposite across the hall
> You haven't swung her since 'way last fall,
> Now trot her home and swing your own,
> And thank your stars the bird ain't flown—
> PROMENADE!

> Hurry up boys and don't be slow
> Meet your pard with a double elbow
> Now ladies bow and the gents bow under
> Take ahold and go like thunder!
> PROMENADE!

Everybody dropped red-faced from laughter and exhaustion.
But after they'd recovered their breath enough, they tried the
graceful old varsoviana, the dance the Spaniards brought into
the Southwest when they came, and which they left behind
them, along with their horses and their sheep and their flaming
bayeta.

The fliers wound up by spending their whole leave at Wide
Ruins. And the parting gesture of one of them, as they were
sitting a last easy hour out in the patio, was to build a little
fire of juniper and pinion twigs between his knees, so he could
take away with him a final whiff of the particularly haunting
lightness of fragrance those wild desert woods make when they
burn. They each went away with a rug they would have liked
even had the rugs been no good. And they weren't particularly.
But they were vegetable dyed.

At that stage Sallie and Bill were taking in any kind of a
rug, so long as it was vegetable dyed. In fact, in their insistence
upon vegetable dyes, they'd overpay, even for an impossible
one, if it were so dyed, and refuse to buy it at all unless it were.

And when a rug came in with a wholly new dye which happened to be pleasing, for that they would pay even more, and hang it in a prominent place on the store wall. Then they would stand talking about it to each other—pointing out the new color admiringly, in the presence of the usual lot of Indians sitting in a row on the loafers' bench at the other side of the store. Thus word of the traders' interest in the new dye would get around through the community, and other rugs would come in with it used one way or another, according to the weaver's spurred fancy.

One day the wife of Moccasin Maker, from far back in the hills, brought in a rug with a red none had ever seen before. It was a rich beautiful red, and she told Sallie she had got it from boiling the red lichen which grows on dead oak trees. None of the weavers in the Wide Ruins area had ever heard of that being tried, and everybody was very excited about it. The Lippincotts sent a sample of the dyed wool and some of the lichen to a friend of theirs who was a research chemist for du Pont. The chemist was as interested in the color as they, tried out its possibilities scientifically, and sent back word that it had a litmus reaction, and by alkali treatment made a true blue. This news was even more rousing than the discovery of the red, for a true blue was difficult to achieve. Indigo was hard to come by any more, and dangerous to use in the hogans. The blue which was made from juniper berries was inclined to be dull, with a grayish cast.

Great preparations began for the formal introduction of a new blue into the desert. Sallie sent word to Moccasin Maker's wife that she would be over on such-and-such a day for the trial, and told her to have the lichen ready. Dead oak trees were not too plentiful, and the red lichen did not always grow on what ones there were. So the whole Moccasin Maker family and all their friends and far relations dropped everything to busy themselves hunting dead oaks with red lichen.

The appointed day rolled around, and Sallie started early. She had to go by horseback because it was a long way, and the Moccasin Maker's hogan was a remote one off the road. She found practically the whole clan gathered, with their lichen, which they had assembled bit by bit, mile by mile. With great flourish and ceremony the lot was dropped into the pot ready over the open fire and began boiling away for dear life. Everybody watched and after so long there appeared that red which was so exciting. Then Sallie poured in the alkali the du Pont chemist had suggested, and Mrs. Moccasin Maker added a hank of yarn, and Sallie began to stir.

Pretty soon she thought the stirring was feeling strange. She lifted up the paddle and the stuff had turned to blue all right—blue jelly! Everybody looked in the pot but they couldn't see a sign of the wool. It had all dissolved. There was dead silence. And then the whole Moccasin Maker clan leaned over and whooped. The Navahos love a joke on themselves, and this one, after all the preparation and fanfare, nearly finished them off.

Sallie didn't know whether she had put in too much alkali or not enough, and she didn't have the courage to try all that again. So although the Wide Ruins rugs had to carry on without benefit of lichen blue, by that time the general idea of vegetable dyes was pretty well established and the experimenting young traders' next step was to begin demanding better weaving to go with the vegetable dyes. After that, clean wool—and then patterns of good simple taste, whether of stripes or not now.

In the history of the Navaho blanket, the plain horizontal stripes were used only up until the 1800's. After that gradually there developed more complicated patterns of rise and fall;

angular, and sometimes with such abstraction as to seem almost modernistic, and yet with an inherent sense of flow about them.

Toward this revival the experimenting rug dealers next went into cahoots with the school up on the hill, offering prizes for the best rug designs made during the children's art period. The children would bring their designs to the store, and gather around while the young white people criticized each design that was submitted, pointing out its good and bad points. Children are not the weavers, except potentially, but the discussion of the designs would be repeated in the hogans, and so put into the thoughts of the women who were the weavers.

Jimmy got the prize in the first of these contests—a shiny toy gun. After that they privately had to rule him out of any part in the competition, for he would have won all the prizes.

But Jimmy was intrinsically aligned with weaving, in a way of his own, for the little Navaho boy painted as his people wove. A weaver will start in on a pattern, working it out in detail as she goes, and when she finishes, although the start of it long ago has been rolled up behind her, the end of the pattern complements its beginning. And that is the way Jimmy painted— not sketching the whole in first, but painting in detail as he went, yet when the picture was finished there was balance and rhythm there.

Sometimes that balance, for him, would extend over a whole series of pictures. Whenever he got a new tube of color, it would seem to tempt all his capacities for use of it, with the use expanding into a resourcefulness he did not know he had until it was touched on and called out. Sometimes it was a combination of color and idea which he used until he had exhausted all its possibilities. Thus one picture of two delicate autumn birch trees with a young brown horse between them, as sensitively made as they, developed into a series whose theme was sapling birch trees with their brown leaves falling. In the second of the series Jimmy bent one of the birches flat across the bottom of the page and put two black turkeys on the branch. In the third picture two birch-gray wolves had been introduced, with one turkey caught and the other fleeing, and a deer fleeing, too. But although flight had grown to be the overtone of the picture rather than delicacy, the birches with their leaves falling were still there.

Weavers take their color and their pattern from things of the earth, and so did the child, essentially. His art took the form of the animals he knew; but the animals carried an emotional expression of things that happened in the life around him, so that they spoke of erring, and attack, and vanity, and ridiculousness, as well as aching beauty. And when his father came back from Colorado Springs a wiser man, Jimmy put it down in color.

Sallie and Bill took Joe along with them on that trip to help them with some horses they were buying—for their own pleasure and also to ride to off-road hogans to see how the weaving was progressing. It was Joe's first trip off the reservation and he got all dressed up for it. He went diked out in an orange silk shirt with silver buttons, beaded armbands, a fringed buckskin vest, a beautiful concha belt, a string of turquoise, and his gray striped morning trousers. He'd doffed his moccasins for orange high-topped shoes with knob toes, and his musty headband had been exchanged for a brand new wide-brimmed black sombrero which he rakishly turned up into a cockade. To top the costume off, he carried his bow and arrows. Joe was highly pleased with his appearance, and in truth he cut quite a swath as the three of them entered the lobby of the Broadmoor Hotel.

But as they climbed aboard the elevator, Joe grew uneasy. They had forgotten to tell him about elevators, and as a door closed on the little room, shutting the man of the desert in, he grew wary. When the little room began moving upward, he turned pea green. Sallie smiled at him reassuringly, and he tried to smile back, but it was a watery smile. When the door opened on a completely different scene than the one they had left, the Indian practically fainted. After that he never ventured on a new floor without first trying out its dependability with the cautious stubbed toe of one shoe.

But by morning he had so far acclimated himself as to go stalking the tame deer around the lake with his bow and arrows —until he was caught at it. Joe proved something of a problem. They kept losing him. Once they found him in the cocktail bar. From what they could piece together from Joe's vague account of it afterward, he'd come upon the stuffed golden pheasant decorating the bar window, and had thought admiringly, What a fine present a feather from that cock's tail would make to take back to the medicine man! So he went in after it.

It is hard to imagine which was the more astonished, the Indian at finding himself in the air-conditioned elegance of the bar, or the head waiter at finding himself confronted by an Indian. But the waiter recovered first, and asked if he had come for a cocktail. Again the Indian paled. Black Magic was afoot! How did that man know he wanted a cock's tail? And then, said Joe in surprise, he didn't get the cock's tail after all, but something in a little glass!

A convivial something, evidently, because when they finally got him located, he was minus his buckskin vest, but was sporting an Elk's badge! Joe, like Ulysses, returned with usage and the world's wide wisdom stored. He came back to his black work shirt, but with the Elk's badge proudly adorning it, and full of knowledge of the out and beyond for Jimmy.

And Jimmy, in that way he did things, slipped away to his drawing table at the back of the store and on a large piece of white paper drew in one corner slowly a few blades of little

grass, which mounted to a single stump in the middle of the page whereon sat one solemn owl. On the other side of the stump were some little grasses again. Jimmy drew wisdom on a stump, and then evidently he thought it over, because in his next picture, on the same kind of paper, he drew a lot of wisdoms on a limb—all facing out, except one incidental owl who sat the other way. But again, he had painted as weavers weave. The limb had started out to be a tree at the right of the page, but finding as he painted the tree upward, in that careful detailed way he worked, that there would not be room on the paper for the tree to go ahead and stand upright, he bent it to a limb. And when it was done, the limb was the part to the pattern that made it whole.

Many things went into the growth of the rug mart at Wide Ruins that couldn't be put down beside a dollar mark in the books—although there was a separate account book started for members of the adult weaving class which the store, in connection with the home economics department at the school, inaugurated.

At first the Navaho women were very uncertain about the propriety of grown-ups going to school. Fortunately, at that time Bill's partner at the carpenter's dance came back to visit them, complete with her doctor's degree. A common meeting was called, with the doctor's-degree owner obligingly allowing herself to be held up as an example that going to school though grown was something that happened even in the best of families. And to encourage the idea, the weaving-class members, whether their credit ordinarily was worth anything or not, were allowed full credit at the store for any weaving materials—soap to wash the wool, wool cards, alum, and the wool itself if the weavers did not have enough of their own. The resulting rugs, then, the traders guaranteed to buy, good or not, although on the whole the results were encouraging.

They even went so far as to up the quality of the natural wool in the native flocks. In a letter home at the beginning of this plan, Sallie wrote: "Tonight we are having a meeting of the range men to talk over introducing a good herd of long-wool Merino sheep in this area. The idea would be to buy the whole present herd from one Navaho—probably Yellow Man —and replace it with these better sheep. Then during the proper season, whenever that is, we would buy a couple of Rambouillet rams and turn them over to Yellow Man. The idea of the plan is to get a good weaving wool started here. We would guarantee to buy all the wool. Since Yellow Man is having a hard time making ends meet, it would help him too."

And through it all, they kept up their fuss about vegetable dyes.

Then, one shouting March day, came the perfect rug! Weaving, they had come to know, was done at unscheduled times all through the several seasons, and at odd places. In the sparse times of summer, the Indians would follow the sheep into the high mountain grazing grounds, and if the winters were bitter, they'd take the sheep to the canyons for shelter. But the crude loom of cedar posts and cross beams was put up in both places, and the woman was never far from it—inside the winter hogan, or sitting with her moccasined feet tucked under her before an outside loom in front of the summer brush camp. And March could be fairly well counted on to bring in the finished products.

This March day, Mrs. Beaver came bringing *the* rug—the rug they'd been working toward. They half unrolled it, and it looked perfect. Everyone was overjoyed—sounds of delight as everyone crowded around. Soft pastels—green, gray, and yellow; a design of simple taste in the re-inspired style began to be revealed as the rug unfolded.

Excitedly they took it into the rug room for a real view.

"The limb was the part that made it whole."

They unrolled it on the floor. And there, blasting out at them from the finish of the pattern, woven into the fabric in black letters, was the assurance, "Vegetable Dye Rug"—in a nasty tone of voice that brooked no argument!

But little by little they were getting it all down pat—pat enough so that they were not being able to supply the demand for the Wide Ruins rugs. And Wide Ruins rugs were beginning to go to distinguished places—officially to Washington, the Laboratory of Anthropology at Santa Fe, the Museum of Modern Art in New York. The Navaho weavers around Wide Ruins were reclaiming their own in the proud threads of The People.

CHAPTER

6

TROUBLE links people with people—trouble is something that is real to everybody; you get down to what's real in yourself at times like that, and find out what's real in other people; people are natural, are themselves, in times of trouble. You get on with people in those times—the essential cuts through the artificial barriers.

Up until the time Jimmy's sister Mary was lost, the relationship between Sallie and Joe was strictly that of mistress and servant, with the handy man performing his duties in the white people's ménage either with a strutting self-importance which would have been annoying had it not been so amusing, or else in a plodding bewilderment. But from the time he came to her in trouble, for help when Mary was lost, it was different.

Mary was several years older than Jimmy, a wildly pretty girl just come into late full bloom. A spirited girl who, Sallie knew from local gossip around the trading post, had been causing her father a good deal of trouble ever since her maturity. Joe put Jimmy to keeping watch on her after school, to see that she did not stop with the boys behind the pinions on her way home. And Jimmy's drawings therefrom took a turn of experience. He drew strange shapeless creatures with oddly lighted eyes like slits, and mouths faintly parted in pleasure, and with big hands like frog feet.

That was the way it had been going ever since Mary's

maturity. The ceremony celebrating that epoch in Mary's life, incidentally, was the first Navaho ceremony in Wide Ruins Sallie and Bill were asked to attend. The invitation came as a gesture of friendliness, and a certain amount of trust, springing, no doubt, from the fact that from the very first the young white traders never had shown surprise or incredulity at the ways of these people of the desert. More, the white people themselves had lifted some of the ancient antagonism between the two races when they asked the grave aloof old Loukaichukai, who bespoke his whole racial dignity, to perform the ceremony at the store which had made the trading post a common meeting ground. But mostly they had been asked because of their interest in and affection for Mary's brother Jimmy— an interest Joe vaguely appreciated without quite understanding.

In the ceremony for Mary, even more than the one at the store, could be felt that acceptance of all simple and natural things which lies at the heart of all Navaho thought. At the natural woman-come time in a girl's life, then, this ceremony is held for her. It is held in frank and simple hope that she grow to be all the woman that woman can be—in body primarily, but as though they know too that a woman is more than a joy of the body, even bearer of children—that woman is the way her eyes look out of her mind: that woman is beauty.

In the legendry which Sallie found behind the present-day ceremony, the winds of the heavens whispered and told the people to hold the first rite of its kind for the daughter of Changing Woman. In that mythical rite the girl was bedecked from matter of the living earth: her sandals, to run for four dawns a race with the east wind, had been painted on her bare feet with ground jet, and ground red stone, and ground white shell. A little of the white shell was sprinkled on her palms as sign of her virginity. And after she had baked bread and shared it as promise of her homemaking, then in that mythical first time, when she had been enhanced with all the jewels of the universe, a great god had thrown his robes on a rainbow for her to lie on, to be beautiful.

In the actual present-day ceremony, it was a wonder to Sallie that Mary lived through it, considering what the same physical ordeal would have done to the ordinary white girl at that tender time of her life. But the first morning of Mary's puberty, news of it was sent around and Mary promptly was taken in hand by the women of the neighborhood—her own mother having died when Jimmy was born. Loukaichukai, the medicine man, was sent for, and in the ensuing four days of ceremony Jimmy, always shy of crowds, but as usual there in the background, grew aware in a new way of the great natural forces that move across his desert, and have since his people's beginning there. Forces caught up in the cadence of the dance, in the insistence and pulse of the chant, in the meaning of color and line—in life itself.

For four dawns Mary ran the traditional race with the east wind—actually she tore a mile and a half to a designated spot east of the hogan, and ran home again, to be set to grinding corn for the ceremonial bread. For three days, all day long, Mary knelt before a stone metate and with another thinner stone, the mano, ground corn without rest. Except for the nights. Nights she lay on a pile of skins and blankets in the place of honor in the hogan, opposite the door which opened to the east. She lay holding a bit of spider web, symbolizing the weaving she would do in her lifetime, a piece of buckskin she would learn to tan with mahogany root, a bean, a corn— things of the earth to keep life, and to make for peace. On her palms was sprinkled a little of the white shell of virginity.

And old Loukaichukai led the chanting which carried the nights into the dawns—wailing chanting, unforgettable in its

urgency, in the terrible pulsing of it out into the darkness—
into the boundless, to its end. If the medicine man was the
center of the ceremony, Mary was its spirit.

During the three days a ceremonial fire of pinion wood,
filling the air with its delicate sweetness, was kept burning
in a pit in front of the Toddy hogan. On the evening of the
third day the fire was allowed to burn to ashes. The pit was
lined with corn husks, with Mary placing the first herself, as
always, toward the east. Then she poured in the gruel which
had been made from the ground corn, to let it bake into the
ceremonial bread. That night she lay bedecked in all the silver
and turquoise she could borrow, to bring her prosperity, while
again the pulses throbbed to the chanting of prayer for her
womanness.

The last night of Mary's ceremony, a wind was rising when
Sallie and Bill went home, and in the morning it was creaking,
as though it had frozen in the night. It was a beautiful morning, but with the dark bloom of winter on it. It was cold.
There were icicles hanging from one of the men's mustaches,
Sallie noticed, and all the men were huddled in their sheepskin coats and blankets, and the women drew their shawls
close. But Mary duly ran her last race—and this morning,
because her long, shining black hair had been washed in
yucca-root suds and was still wet when she started, she came
back with it frozen in solid strands. The women took her
inside long enough to thaw out her hair, then she emerged
to the cold of the outside again.

There was no god to cast down a rainbow for Mary to lie
on, but all the men took off their sheepskin coats, and lifted
the blankets from their shoulders, and threw them on the
ground for her. Then they made a pile of their sombreros,
toward the invariable east. Mary lay face down on the coats,
facing the sombreros, with her arms up over her head, while

Little Woman, the oldest woman of her clan, knelt, and with her old hands mysterious, went all over the young girl's body to make it straight, to make it beautiful.

With that, the ceremony was over. The medicine man said, "Hozone"—Peace. The bread baking in the fire pit turned out to be a loaf big as a washtub. Everybody ate a little of it, and went home.

The next news Sallie expected to hear of Mary was that she was ill of pneumonia or exhaustion, or both. But that very afternoon she was in the store, divested of her ceremonial finery and in her limp cotton dress again, but with her new role about her still mysteriously. With her clear dark skin and almond face, and almond eyes with a sensuous fullness over them, her mouth with a fullness too, she seemed a half warm young animal, and yet something lovely and untouchable, too.

Most of the crowd from the ceremony had drifted on over to the store. Jimmy was there, as usual back out of the way, behind the stove. The old medicine man, a little out of role, calmly was having a bottle of pop and a nickel's worth of cup cakes. And over by the long counter a young man was talking softly to two young Navaho women, and spinning a silver dollar the length of the counter.

He had on a torn blue shirt under his fringed buckskin vest, and was so far modern as to have a haircut. But even so his black hair hung nearly to his shoulders and was flung back from his high-boned face by a dark red band. There was more outward arrogance about him even than most—with an air of the commanding man that a woman throws away heaven itself for the privilege of yielding to. Had he been a man of the white race, he would have been designated as a bachelor, but since that is a state incredible to the Navaho, their language doesn't bother with the term.

As Mary came into the store, Sallie saw him turn, leisurely.

Then quickly he swept Mary from foot to head with a bold bright glance—so bright as their eyes met across the crowd, and held, that life was between them. Just for an instant. Then, insolently, he turned back to the two women on either side of him. His lean brown hand reached for the silver dollar spinning to a stop, and he set it spinning again, and he and the two women laughed. The laughter, as the talking had been, was low, like laughter after the lights are turned out.

Mary flushed. The flush came slowly, as though from an acid spilled and spreading in her chest. Her eyes angered, from that slow spreading burning. And she flipped around, and had a very gay time with a crowd of her own.

That was the beginning of Joe's troubles with her. Her liveliness grew too much for him to cope with, and she grew too cannily elusive for Jimmy to keep track of. Even the public disciplining from the Tribal Council, which Joe himself called, did not stop her—it didn't even slow her down. Finally in desperation, after about two years of trying to keep the girl in hand and failing, Joe sent Mary away to the convent school where occasionally the Navaho girls of the Wide Ruins community went. He sent her to learn some of the control he himself seemed unable to teach her. All Navaho parents love their children and Joe, in his way, was an especially loving parent. He wanted good things for his children. And, with his particular addiction to the white people's way, mixed as it was with the Navaho trait of putting trouble behind him and forgetting it, he presently forgot why he'd sent her there, and grew proud of his daughter being in a white convent school.

Mary stayed in the school a while, and then she left. The news came by telephone—a call for one Joe Toddy, father of Mary Toddy. Joe was terrified by the call—not by the possible import of the summons, his mind had not gone that far yet—but just at the idea of facing personally the strange black instrument on the house wall. Even when the telephone hung silent, Joe always made a great big circle around the mysterious thing, as though that were one way of keeping out of the trouble he always seemed to suspect it of being able to cause.

And now, at its actually calling for him, he was stricken. Sallie tried to show him what to do, and jockeyed him into position. The strong, square-cut Indian held the receiver gingerly a good six inches from his ear and stared a long slow time in fascinated horror at the mouthpiece.

"Say 'hello,'" prompted Sallie.

Joe took a deep breath that drew up his limp black silk shirt over his barrel chest enormously and quavered, "Hello." And when a voice in the little black thing he held at his ear answered, with a touch of impatience because the Sister at the other end of the line had been waiting, that was too much for Joe. He stood propping himself up, staring, his mouth opening and closing soundlessly. In the end, Sallie had to act as go-between.

The long and short of it was that Mary had run away. The report came edgily. Obviously the months with the untamed young Navaho girl who had not the slightest desire or intention of being tamed in the strictures of a convent school had been something of a struggle. And now the school was calling to report that, so far as they knew, she'd started across the desert for home, and to ask if she had returned yet.

She had not. Nor did she. Joe waited, with his dried leather forehead wrinkling even deeper than ever, and his long hair draggling at his temples worriedly. Joe waited three days, in the due course of tradition, before he took any actual steps in the matter. And then, on the fourth day, four being always the prescribed number, in the time element as in all things else, he started out to look for her. He scoured the hogans of all their possible friends and relations where he hoped Mary might be.

But no one had seen Mary. Sallie called the school again, but the girl had not returned there. No one knew anything about Mary.

Nobody knew, and so, not knowing, superstitious fear began to take hold. There was a Navaho man in the vicinity of the neighboring trading post at Klagatoh whom the other Navahos feared with a fear almost worse than that of death. He was called the Werewolf. He was believed to be able to turn himself into a wolf at night, and raid their flocks. Also he was supposed to do the horrible and dig up dead bodies and rob them of their jewels. And it was true that he was unaccountably rich in sheep, and it probably also was true that he robbed graves, for he possessed a great amount of silver and jewelry, some of which was unique and recognizable by the family hall mark. But since the fear of the werewolf goes back as far in the Navaho tribal tradition as the fear of witchcraft itself, any white person could understand how a local witch could exploit that fear indefinitely and unbeatably.

But the fear of this particular witch, that increased now with Mary in mind, was worse than that. The real terror of the nocturnal wanderer was an unshakable notion that he killed his human victims and devoured them—and the victims of the werewolf were usually women.

The belief in the werewolf is a common and ancient one with the Navahos—the belief in a human wolf, in a man disguised in animal skins who goes about at night practicing witchcraft. Witchcraft, anywhere that it is believed, feeds upon human fears and contentions. And sexual pathologists put down this particular idea of a man changing himself into an animal for cannibalistic purposes to the desire to devour both the loved and the hated objects, and see in the werewolf's lust the symbolism of repressed sexual aggression.

And in that mad, wild way that thought of the worst seems

to spring involuntarily to the human mind, horror tales began
springing up like wildfire around the trading post—of werewolves and werebears meeting in the night and traveling so
fast none can catch them but leaving tracks like paws, and
looking down into hogan roof holes and knowing how to
make people sick. Sometimes the wolf would knock four times,
or sometimes the people inside the hogan would only hear the
mud falling from the roof and know it was the wolf there.
But always, with or without warning, the wolf appeared with
paralyzing slowness to its victims—peeking around the corner
of the door blanket, or letting just its eyes show for a while
over the hole in the roof, and then slowly the rest of him.
Wolves caused sickness. That was the way tuberculosis came.
A wolf would throw something down onto the hogan fire to
make it flare and stink, and the evil fumes would get into
the lungs.

If they caught their victims out in the open they would
throw a powder on them, which would kill them slowly. It
was a powder made from digging into graves for the tongue
of a girl and the finger of a man.

Usually the young traders tried to help straighten out the
problems around the post without offering any radical changes
in the way of Navaho natural life. But this time, because Joe
was so distraught, they tried to tell him that there was no such
thing as witchcraft—that if people died from such practices it
was their own fear which killed them. That might be so. But
there was no arguing the fact that the man from Klagatoh *did*
sometimes dress himself up in skins at night and attack women
—and that it was a screen for sexual abnormalcy was no less
reason to worry about the missing Mary. Nor did it help to
point out to the frantic Joe that the people who were spreading
these tales, taking such lustful zest in them, were merely mir-

roring their own minds, finding release for their distorted impulses in stories of others' outright activities along such lines.

Joe was a father worried about his daughter, and so, when he came to the house one night after days of futile search for Mary, and stood at the door with need in his eyes and in his broken speech, Sallie went with him. She went to take the place of Mary's mother in a star-gazing ceremony to try to find out actually what was happening, or had happened, to the girl.

The strangeness and weirdness of such a request is something you do not think of before need as great as Joe's. Bill had left that morning for business in California, so Sallie set off over the hill alone with the handy man—the only two people in all the vastness of that far-starred night with the hills like strong shadows—until they reached the hogan, and there was Loukaichukai waiting, and Jimmy trying to get himself awake from his bed of skins on the floor.

All during the ceremony the little boy tried to keep awake and take part, because he had been worried about his sister too. Sallie knew, although he hadn't said so, except by helping to try to find her, and in the reflection that the stories about werewolves had found in the one drawing he'd made during the time. He'd drawn a gray wolf with slit eyes and a red tongue in its open mouth, ready to set out.

So Jimmy sat up, but he kept nodding sleepily to the side, and falling over against Sallie's shoulder. He'd wake up with a start, and look at Sallie sideways to see if she had noticed, then he would frown and inch over toward his father. But pretty soon he'd be back asleep on her shoulder.

Meanwhile Loukaichukai was setting up shop at the back of the hogan. He laid out his blanket and sat down, facing the east. Then from his medicine bundle he gave Sallie and

Joe each some mystic flints, which they passed back and forth with high seriousness as he chanted. Finally Sallie was left holding all the flints while Joe and Loukaichukai went outside and the medicine man chanted to the stars. Loukaichukai's shadow showed in the moonlit doorway. His long shadow-arms raised four times, and each time the arms would rise, his voice would rise too.

Whether the sagacious old Loukaichukai really had the occult power of star reading—holding an ancient faith known long before the star of Bethlehem was followed—or whether he merely was wise in the ways of humans and going on a hunch of his own about Mary's whereabouts, Sallie could not have said. But at any rate when the two men came back in and sat down again, Loukaichukai sat thinking deep thoughts very silently.

At last he spoke. He said he saw a mesa with a hogan on it, and that there was a bright light in the hogan, so Mary was all right. Joe was so glad to hear about that bright light he almost cried. There would have been no cheerful light had the werewolf from Klagatoh been concerned in the matter. Joe asked Sallie if she would go with him to get Mary, and she did. Bright and early the next morning they started out in the truck to find the mesa Loukaichukai had described.

It was June, with June's gentleness. It had rained in the night—not one of those destructive rains that wash away trails and leave hillsides gutted, although it had begun unexpectedly —the first plap of it on the roof was like a silver dollar dropping. But after that it had come easily, gently, slowly to its whole power, and then was quietly over. After the rain of the night the day now was clear. The sky was a light, shining blue, and white clouds rimmed all the hills and the deep green pines looked clean. In the sunny morning the wind was easy and fresh and all the flowers of the desert were in bloom. Yellow snowberries like forsythia, and desert primroses, and masses of little white flowers called Baby's Bed because it is used for stuffing cradle board mattresses, and a little low red flower that grows all summer long. Mountain mahogany was in bloom on the rocky slopes, and all sorts of cactus flowers so brilliant Sallie was tempted to gather them in armfuls—but she didn't; some flowers know how to protect themselves. And everywhere the yucca plants were blooming—long stalks of creamy flowers that grew high.

Yucca flowers come in their own time. On one center stem there may be one bud opening a little, but with the heart still tightly and widely enclosed. Another a little farther down the stem stands like an ivory cup, reserved. Another an upright bowl, spreading to hold everything. The last tilts with its own weight, catching and holding loosely its own heartfall.

Late in the June morning Sallie and Joe came finally to the mesa Loukaichukai had said he had seen in the stars. And a cedar-post hogan was in the middle of it, as though in the middle of sunny space, and sure enough, there was Mary. She was sitting in the shade of a pinion tree at one side of the hogan, and the young man of the arrogant manner that day at the store was lying beside her, his hands clasped under his head.

Mary was well, obviously, as Loukaichukai had said she was, and happy, as though she had been sent up high and happy out of her wildness. But evidently that was different from the well-being Joe had expected to find. Virginity is no more to be expected long in the Navaho way of life than celibacy, but nonetheless he had been thoroughly frightened and worried about her, and now he was thoroughly angry. He leaped from the truck and pulled a long yucca stalk for a whip to beat her, and started toward her with a beginning of tongue lashing which brought the young man to her side with a few words to say himself. But he didn't need to. Mary stood very straight before her father, looking him straight in the eye, with her own eyes big and black now. She stood there ramrod straight, standing her ground—and Sallie knew Joe loved her for it! For the first time the girl looked tall and slender, and she was beautiful. Sallie saw that Joe scarcely was able to finish out his sternness with her. But something in his faltering then told her how concerned he and Jimmy had been about her, and her voice warmed, and her eyes, and she said that she'd go home. Then she turned to take leave of the man. It was only a matter of their standing and looking at each other a moment.

A long moment. For Mary one of quiet, of all-embracing peace; a lushness, a fullness of body and spirit was in her look, that of having given everything to someone who could command her and finding it enough—the whole answer to her reason for being. And strangely, the arrogant one was looking down at her with almost a humility, a need of her.

Mary went, but she went looking back, as though she really were not going. And Joe sat in the truck holding the yucca whip a little helplessly, scattered. He would beat her when he got her home, but he sat holding the whip as though he were not sure after all that it was something he should do—as though he would be breaking into a pattern that was taking its own rightful shape.

But thereafter there was a change in his attitude toward Sallie and Bill. It was as though now he knew they were people he could count on. That they would be there for him, in his times of bewilderment—in amusing times of his complete frustration before the machine world of their kind. And finding they were friends, who let his interests be their interests in his time of troubling over his daughter, he came to trust them about his son. Beyond his own wondering he trusted them, by earnestly trying now not to lead Jimmy, but to follow him. And if he could not quite follow, at least try to recognize that the child had the kind of mind that goes places only one can go. In blind faith Joe began accepting Sallie's stand in the matter from the start—that Jimmy's mind be given freedom to go his own way, without making him aware of the small frightening barriers he didn't know about yet, nor should.

So that Jimmy, with a knowledge beyond his years, for age has nothing to do with directness of mind and heart, went on unhindered straight to the core of things. He painted green-gray hungry coyotes on cold green paper, making the coyotes out of angular lines. Jimmy painted a young horse a salmon color with bushy black mane and tail not like a horse's at all, but like a fox's, with a wicked glee in its black eye and kicking another horse for no reason except the vicious need of the lusty young for hate. He painted two tawny mountain goats on a tawny background, grazing at peace, when mountain goats are not tawny but peace was the whole of it. Jimmy painted two strong birds flying to come together on a gnarled tree on a tired piece of lonely earth.

And Joe would only ask humble permission to bring his friends into the studio at the back of the store to see his son's work, and then stand pointing a square finger at it proudly, with a pride that would grow baffled as at something beyond him. Nevertheless he no longer tried to get Jimmy to change the color or the shape of the things he painted to bring them back to the world. Rather the finger would fall wonderingly before what he pointed at, as pointing fingers do before something impellingly honest, at something unconsciously natural. From then on Joe was like a parent who watches a child playing some intent game which only the child knows, the parent not asking for fear of spoiling it.

CHAPTER

7

"JOE," Sallie asked him one day, "does Jimmy like me?" The handy man looked up from the latchstring for the patio gate he was cutting from a piece of rawhide and nodded his head vigorously. "Sure. Jimmy like you lots."

"But he never talks to me."

There came a long silence. Joe slowly went on with his cutting of the leather thong. When he had it the right size, he doubled up his knife and put it away in his levi pocket. Then he straightened, and his chest under his limp black work shirt heaved up, and let down, in a great sigh.

"He no talk to me either," he admitted sadly.

The little boy was shutting everybody out of his shy world, it seemed, even his father. Joe put the thong through the hole in the gate, to tie it to the latch on the other side.

The gate was a small wooden one in the center of a high stone wall which divided the house patio from the trading-post yard. Actually the wall had been put up as protection against the sandstorms which the Lippincotts had found, to their discomfort, began the first of May and lasted almost to the end of that month. The sand didn't blow all that time—just most of it. When they had first taken over Wide Ruins there had been what was supposed to be a sandstorm wall —chicken wiring stretched across the middle of the yard, bolstered by pieces of roofing iron; and the paper cartons and tin cans which the Navahos had thrown away from the camps they used to make in the trading-post yard, had been piled against it by the wind. Besides being an eyesore, it proved inadequate for its purpose, and they had torn it down and built a new one.

The new wall was a scientifically gauged height of nine feet and built of stone. The stone had been cut from the canyon a ways from the trading post, and it would take several hundred years of weathering before it quite matched the stone of the old house, but in the meantime it kept out the sandstorms. It had been put up as functional wall, but as it turned out it was a wall which divided two worlds. On the patio side of it was a modern world, in which the Lippincotts lived as they would have in any other part of the country. But on the other side the world was primitive still. A wildly colorful world, in which a pristine life went on essentially as it had from its beginning, remarkably untouched by change.

This contrast was one which especially struck visitors to the place. Wide Ruins was beginning to attract visitors—family, and friends who came out of interest and curiosity, and people who happened upon it accidentally, such as the one who nearly got swept down the wash on the other side of the trading post one stormy night.

Storms were particularly dramatic affairs in the desert. From Wide Ruins they could be seen piling up a long way off, and drawing in closer and closer until the place was drenched with rain and the wash was running full of red water. Those rains brought out the smells of the desert—the strong smell of earth, and the tang of sage freshened. But they were disastrous rains, so far as roads were concerned. At the foot of the hill where the road came in from the highway it always washed out completely, leaving the bridge the Lippincotts had built there hanging in mid air—nothing coming or going from it, just a white bridge all by itself, looking foolish. On the other side of the trading post the wash which crossed the road on into the desert filled rapidly with a wall of water which sometimes rose as much as seven feet in half an hour.

Strangers in that part of the country, not knowing how swiftly waters can rise in desert canyon beds and gulleys and washes, more than once had been known to choose some such spots for camp sites. They would choose them because they looked dry and were sheltered on either side by high sand banks or rocks—and then, in a sudden rain that would send water rushing between those banks, like water sent out to overturn the earth, they would drown.

Ordinarily, after two years in the desert, the Lippincotts went about their affairs with little concern for wetness or dryness, or calmness or storm. They had come to know the country around them by horseback in any kind of weather— the country that changed in character with every half mile, first the rolling desert and sage immediately around the trading post, juniper forests beginning just back of the horse corral, the land rising and turning trackless up through rocky mountain sides, coming out to a high place that had the canyon below, and beyond the mountains. On days with a stormy light to them the junipers took on the same olive-green cast as the saddle slickers. Winter nights had the whole clean wide world in the first sharp breathful—the horses would feel them, too, and go pounding across the hard sand like free thunder.

When weather was so bad the outside world left the people on the reservation to themselves, they still would get together for dances, or skating on somebody's stock pond, plowing through the roads without giving the matter two thoughts. But nobody who knew ever fooled with a rushing arroyo.

This particular dusk which brought them an unexpected visitor, the rain had fallen like a steel curtain, let down suddenly close in front of the trading post. As they stood in the doorway watching, it let up. It did not stop, but it thinned enough to see through. And like something in a blurred film, they saw car lights zigzagging their way down the muddy road leading in from the desert. Whoever it was must be a stranger, to be heading for the water-filled wash which crossed the road just beyond the post. They sent Joe running to warn him. The driver of the car said afterward he saw a Navaho waving to him, but thought the Indian was just being friendly, and waved back. The car lights made a sudden drop off, and disappeared out of sight.

All hands at the post went rushing dramatically to the rescue—which ended up with everybody fishing everybody else out of the wash. But among the lot was the driver of the car. Even that soon, by the time they got to the wash edge, the car was floating rapidly downstream sideways, with the driver on top, stripping and getting ready to swim for it. He turned out to be a professor of anthropology from Harvard, whom Sallie had met before, under different circumstances.

For him, the surprise of meeting again, and here, lost none of its shock as the evening went on. Sallie's old cook from home had had to leave, regretfully, because she had liked Wide Ruins and hoped to come back. But she had been replaced by Mary from Texas, as placid as a piece of her own deft dough. Cooking not only was this one's occupation—it was her passion. Her idea of good reading was the cookbook, her idea of an afternoon off was to go through the food markets in Gallup. Her life was dated by recipes. "I learned to make hollandaise sauce in October 1927," she would remember dreamily, as though that were a pleasant and staying thing for one to have in one's background. An unexpected guest for dinner only added to her quiet joys.

A little dazedly the Harvard professor sat down to a dinner out in the middle of nowhere which began with a clear soup and hot crackers; went through a fried chicken Maryland style course; was touched up with a salad the secret of whose particular dressing Mary had learned in the summer of '31; and topped off by chocolate cake and banana mousse—"banana mush," as Bess called it when Sallie asked her what was for dessert.

The little Navaho maid went back and forth with the serving—adding her especial smack to it—her quick black eyes making sure that everything at the table was as should be. Then, when the "mush" was duly served, Bess stood and swung her arms zestfully and slung at the assembly, "Whatchoo want to drink—Coca-Cola, root beer, lemon pop, or sarsaparilla?"

This was a ritual Bess never could resist. The Navahos are ardent drinkers of any kind of pop, and the idea of having such a range of choice from the store next door always got the best of her. The man from the East didn't believe he wanted any sarsaparilla with his mousse, thank you, but he still was so flabbergasted by the general variety of choice, he chose some exotic liqueur to go with his demitasse—just for the rarity of the whole idea.

And the visitors who more and more were finding Wide Ruins, and coming back, were buying Jimmy's pictures. Sallie sold them for very little—never more than a dollar and usually for much less. But everyone who saw them wanted to buy them, and both Sallie and Bill felt that a little money, without too much of it to spoil him, might be a good idea. Since he went to the white people's school, and one way or another as he went along no doubt would continue to have contact with the white people's world, it seemed well that he learn something of the value of the white people's dollar.

Navahos, by nature, have all the disregard for money that the Spartans had, who had proved the nuisance of it by making it of iron so that as much as a hundred dollars would have had to be hauled around in wagons. Almost no money ever changed hands across the Wide Ruins store counters. Pelts, wool, rugs from the wool, nuts, turquoise they dug from the mountains—this was their money produced when it was needed. In return they got food, clothing, hay, sheep, salt, raw silver which they hammered into jewelry and brought back again to trade. Those who aspired to be men of substance, or who had been born into that class, came by that position according to the number of horses they owned. But the horses were the wild ones, descended from the ones left by the Spaniards, and were already there in the Navaho hills, needing only to be caught and tamed.

And Jimmy himself seemed to pay no attention to the small pieces of money which came his way. Sallie would put them on the corner of his drawing table, but he would not seem to notice. In time, however, they would disappear. His first wealth in cash money he spent for a sack of pink cup cakes with cocoanut frosting and a box of crackerjack. Then he began regularly buying milk for his little half-brother. This made Joe very proud. Jimmy's little brother was practically the only baby in the Wide Ruins district who had milk to drink. But when his first check came in, Jimmy made a real investment—and this was quite contrary to the habits of his kind.

Navahos, as a race, are notoriously improvident. They are squanderers more than they are lazy. It is true they cannot be hurried into work, any more than they can be hurried out of their pastoral and nomadic life into one of schools and machinery. Nor will a Navaho do any kind of work until he decides for himself that he wants to. But even when he does bend his proud back to labor, the returns are promptly spent on something to be immediately enjoyed. Occasionally a Navaho condescends to pick up a shovel and help in the government work of ditches and reservoirs across his desert, but any return for that is gone before the check is cold. If it is the increase of his property—sheep or horses—on which he has expended his efforts, then he trades that stock for something else he wants. Some of the Navahos around Wide Ruins were well fixed in this kind of property. Big Tom Gun had a thousand sheep and a great many horses. But there were others, like Yellow Man, who only worked harder and got poorer. People like Yellow Man knew that everything was hard to get—even little things had to be worked for. But also, people like Yellow Man with only a pittance spent it. That was one of the responsibilities which the young traders felt they had in the community —seeing that people who they knew could not afford to spend their money foolishly, take out at least a reasonable amount of trade in goods which would tide the family over until the next surge of affluence. But rich or poor, as a race the Navahos do not look ahead. Jimmy, however, put his first sum into something whose returns would keep coming in.

This was the money which resulted from a public exhibit of his paintings. From the day Sallie and Bill had found the shy little boy scratching out a picture on a stone, the child had showed he had his own way of doing things, and in the two years since then, had strengthened in it. With his growth in the use of color, he came to use it more and more toward the feel of his subject rather than its fact. He painted blue rabbits and yellow porcupines and horses with tails like black foxes. The desert animals which Jimmy painted always were more suggestion than portraiture. And the instinctive sense of rhythm and balance of his pictures was growing with his increased use of it. At first the balance had been gained by the vibration of one color against another. But lately the child

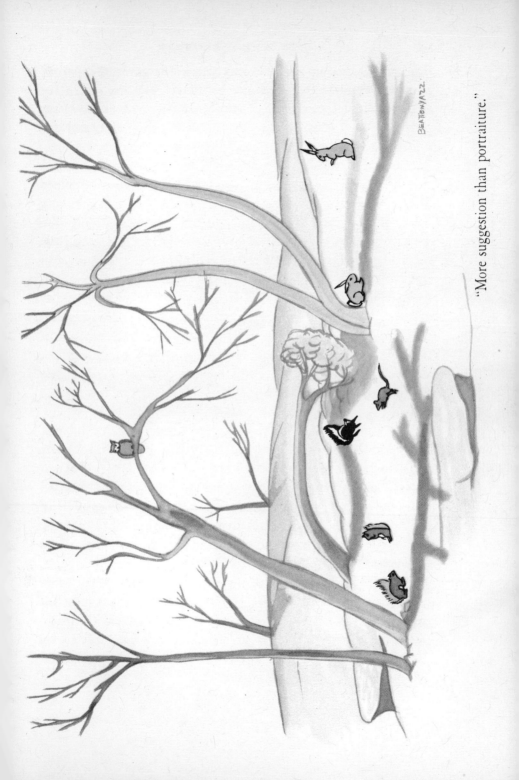

"More suggestion than portraiture."

had come into the use of line as well as the use of light. And in that way one thing pulled on to another with him; the combination of the two was carrying him headlong now.

In the latest picture Sallie had found left on his drawing table, he had used two-toned pastel swings of very short lines. The lines made a plane, with a great rock in it; and lying on the rock, curving the lines of its body up over it to the edge, was a long mountain lion, waiting—looking down on two un-suspecting rabbits of the same ironically sweet tones.

Jimmy had his own way and he seemed ready now to go forward with it. Sallie never did any more directing of the child than to see that he had materials to work with, and when Bill had rebuilt the store, he had made space in it for Jimmy to have just for himself. But interest in the child's work was mounting through the post's visitors, and when the oppor-tunity came for him to have a public showing in an exhibit at the State Museum at Springfield, Illinois, Sallie packed up some of his pictures and sent them, and all that she sent were sold—for the small sums she'd marked on the back.

Jimmy did not go to the exhibit. He never had been off the reservation. And Sallie could not tell how much he compre-hended of what she told him about it, since he never talked with her. But she told him that his paintings had been put in a great big building, something like the buildings at Wide Ruins, only much larger, and that people had come from all around to look at his pictures. She told him the people had liked his pictures, and had sent him some money for them. The little boy said nothing, although he ducked his head and grinned that grin of his.

And he paid not the slightest attention, apparently, to the check she tried to hand him. It had come by mail on a Satur-day morning, while he was out in his studio at the back of the store. Since it was his first check, and she knew it would be an experience for him, she took it in to him excitedly. But Jimmy just went right on with the picture he was painting. Finally, slowly, without lifting his head to look up, he reached out his left hand for the little piece of paper and took it— while with his right hand he went on with a careful line he was painting! Then Sallie explained to him how that check could mean money, that if he would sign his name on the back of it and take it into the store Bill would give him the amount that was written on it.

Again the little boy only listened, with no reply. But as soon as he had finished with the line he was making he cleaned his paint brushes and put them away and got a fresh stack of paper and spent the rest of the day practicing writing his name. Every once in a while he would go to the store door and look in and see how the gallery was. Along about closing time, when the store was fullest, Jimmy sallied out from his back room, check in hand, made his way over to the cash register, and while Indians craned curiously, Jimmy, with a fine flourish, wrote his name on the back of the check. Then he and his father went proudly off up over the hill together.

The check was for eleven dollars, and Jimmy bought chickens with it. Sallie and Bill kept chickens, so Jimmy bought chickens. The next day Jimmy did not go to school. When Sallie quizzed Joe about this, he told her that Jimmy had been worried about his chickens.

"Roost in tree, wid owls," Joe had relayed to Sallie anxiously. "Make foony eggs maybe."

So Jimmy had stayed home from school to build a chicken house, as nearly like the Lippincotts' as he could, from packing crates.

About a week after that Joe came to Sallie again about Jimmy. The little boy had been sick in the night.

"Eggs—" Joe had told her. "Fling 'em oop."

It seemed that Jimmy had watched, and noticed that in the store eggs went by dozens. So he had carefully saved up his first dozen eggs, and then sat solemnly down and eaten them— and been violently ill.

Jimmy still never talked to the two young white people— but he was following them, in everything.

Joe, after his admission that Jimmy never talked to him either, was going on a little bewilderedly with his work on the latchstring. He put it through the hole in the gate and tied it to the latch on the other side, and it was done, and Sallie wandered around the patio, seeing how the first of summer was doing.

The summer was beginning very well. When they had first come to Wide Ruins this part of the general yard in front of the trading post had been a dump heap. Both the Indians who came to the store and the old men who had lived in the house evidently had thrown things out as they were through with them. Tin cans and trash soggy with years. Sallie had Joe haul the junk off by the wheelbarrow load, and now there were yellow roses that smelled like cinnamon, and white silver moon roses and ramblers. There was a mint bed around the bird bath, and nasturtiums had followed the jonquils. There were young junipers against the new wall, to tie the land-scaping in with the junipers and tamarisk which had been there before, and which the Lippincotts had left as they were. It was good growing ground in the patio.

"Raise 'em up seeds, grass, anything, yiss—" Joe had commented vaguely.

Joe was not too keen a gardener, true to his race. In fact he had to be corraled into helping with it at all. Sallie herself was not a devoted gardener. But there was a satisfaction in putting something in the ground and knowing it wouldn't have any better sense than to take root and grow and bloom, even while half the world on the other side of the ocean was starting in on destruction. It was good to watch things grow. Watching a child grow was even better.

There was a slight movement to the new latch string. The gate in the wall was being slowly opened. Sallie looked up to see Jimmy come into the patio—shyly, from the other side.

CHAPTER

8

AT THE beginning of the summer Jimmy had seemed ready to go forward. But as the summer went on, he went backward instead. And it was not until the day of the Thanksgiving Turkey Shoot that he even got to sure enough ground to start again. Something had happened.

The two artists from Munich who had come to Wide Ruins early that summer, and become so entranced with the place they stayed until fall, were especially interested in Jimmy. The idea of a little boy, and more, an untrained child of the primitives, painting the animals of his desert in the particular way he did, fascinated them. In his painting of a timidly happy mauve-colored doe frolicking gently under a bare oak tree, it surprised them that he instinctively should know to bend one bough of the tree to repeat the curve of the doe's back. The interest in Jimmy's pictures did not stop with the first glance but went on, in shapes re-echoing, and colors repeating. His colors were not true to their original subject, but they were true to each other.

With these natural beginnings, the artists enthusiastically undertook the child's training. They showed him how to use their equipment, which was infinitely more complete than Jimmy's own. His equipment consisted of some ordinary paint brushes and the usual water colors, and Sallie would continue to bring him a fresh drawing or painting pad whenever she went to Gallup—although he seldom used them any more. He preferred choosing his own paper, from odds and ends around, as they happened to appeal to him. He cut a piece of brown wrapping paper from the store a size he wanted, and tried four red-brown astounded deer on it, all with their antlers turned disapprovingly toward one red-brown deer blandly in the middle. On the torn-off side of a carton he painted a soft black bear holding a gray rock, with a Mother Hubbard apron quality to its kindly eye and thin smile. He painted a blue rabbit on the back of an advertisement from the Liberty Music Shop, which he rescued from the Lippincot s' wastebasket. From that he went in for blue rabbits for a while—which was slightly disconcerting.

But the artists generously insisted upon the shy silent little boy using their paper, from their own good stock of it. They showed him how to use their special brushes, and their palettes and their easels, and they showed him about light. Jimmy's own light was a shaded bulb which Sallie tried to keep adjusted to a proper height, although it was a futile attempt. No matter how the light fell, Jimmy sat practically on top of the paper, his dark head bent close over his drawing, and his hair falling down over his face, so that whatever he was doing was completely shaded by his head and hair. But the artists showed him about the proper use of it, and shifted him about from place to place. As they went along with their own work, they talked to him about what they themselves had learned.

Jimmy grew confused, bewildered. The paintings he tried to do in the ways he was being taught were no good. They were no good by the orthodox standards, and whatever had been in him of his own seemed being driven out of him. By the end of summer he was not painting at all.

In desperation Sallie tried putting up on the wall around his work table some of his own funny little drawings, which no one else had taught him to do. At first this did not seem to reach him. School opened, and his troubles continued.

One of the teachers at the Wide Ruins school that fall was there, according to her own explanation which she always gave elegantly, "to learn the Navahos to speak English." She had a yen for big words. "Isn't it wonderful," she would marvel ecstatically, of the breadth of view from the schoolhouse hill, "how you can conceive at such great distances out here?"

She and Jimmy did not get along. In the art periods, instead of dutifully filling in with crayon the traced pictures of Dutch windmills and apples and pears, the little boy just sat. No sharpness or blunt force could make him lift a crayon to fill in those pictures. Since he could no longer paint in his own way, there seemed something in him now that would not let him touch another's.

The teacher complained at the store about Jimmy Toddy's wilfulness. It was not Sallie's province, for the trading post officially had nothing to do with the school. But she couldn't stand by indifferently. Even under the hands of able and well-intentioned artists, she had been seeing that Jimmy had to do things his own way for them to be right to him. And this matter of direct copying she had fought out a long time ago, with Joe.

When Jimmy first began painting, his father was so proud that he began picking out the most likely of the Lippincotts' magazines, for Jimmy to copy the pretty pictures. Most Navaho children have marked artistic ability, and Sallie was not sure that Jimmy had more than others. But from the beginning he had had his own approach, and whatever might or might not come of it, she felt his right to that approach should be respected.

"But Jimmy has to draw his own pictures, Joe!" she had

tried to explain to the handy man. "If he draws pictures someone else has done, he won't grow up to be a good artist—or a
good man. And you want him to be a good man, don't you?"

Joe had nodded vaguely, not quite seeing the connection.
But sullenly, in the end, he had relinquished the magazine
idea.

Jimmy's teacher proved to be not so amenable. Fortunately
for Jimmy, however, her reign was too short-lived to have
much effect on him. One day she found herself with no pupils
to teach. The day before she had put a bowl of goldfish in
the window, to make the schoolroom more cheery. The most
elementary book on the legends by which the everyday lives
of the Navahos are still intricately governed, could have told
her that fish were once Navaho ancestors. Consequently when
the children went home to their hogans, big-eyed with the
news that the teacher had their ancestors trapped in a little
bowl up at the school, angry and frightened parents yanked
their children out of that place of evil power in a hurry.

The teacher who replaced her was more happily aligned
with the plans for the educational advancement which was beginning to be made in other parts of the reservation. There was
an earnest movement afoot to try to correct the past mistakes
in an educational program which the Indian Rights Association had pronounced "bad faith, blundering, a tragic mess."
The Indian Service—with the help of the Bureau of American
Ethnology, of anthropological scholars trained in the understanding of Navaho culture, and of a few of the Navahos
themselves who had gone off the reservation for their training
and come back—was now trying to give the Navaho children
a kind of education which would adapt itself to their natural
life.

Children were being taught their own language classically,
as well as how to speak English, and to write and figure. They

were being taught about stock control and desert farming. Home economics lessons were given in two ways—in the hogans, using the foods at hand and cooking them over open fires; and then comparatively, in the scientific kitchens of the schools. And each home economics class adopted a current crop of the ever-present foundlings, to find out from practical experience about the proper care and feeding of infants. They made cradles out of barrel slats, industriously painted them pink and blue, and put brown babies in them. The boys were taught to make furniture—to augment the pile of blankets, the loom, and the anvil which were the only furnishings their people usually bothered with. With the new teacher's arrival, the trading post and the school began working together in the general community interests, and the governmental program at Wide Ruins went ahead by leaps and bounds.

There, as in all schools on the reservation, attendance was not compulsory. But Jimmy was fairly faithful in it—although against his inclinations. School in any form was hard on him. But he endured it, with his characteristic silence. Indeed the new teacher was beginning to think the little boy *couldn't* talk until one rainy noon, having lunch at the school, she appealed to the children for help with the menu, and Jimmy spoke up firmly and decidedly.

"No spinach!" His boldness scared him to death, and he spent the rest of the day in retirement in a corner.

So far as his art went, the new teacher was being understanding enough. But she had laid down one rule which was definitely and personally objectionable to him. To keep order as the children marched out at noons and recesses, she made them go out two by two. To Jimmy's intense mortification it was his lot to walk with the little Belai girl—unless he could knock down enough people and get to the head of the line, to his friend, the Shorty boy, before the teacher noticed. The little Belai girl had a warm heart but also unfortunately she had warts on her hands and her loving nature always seemed to prompt her to squeeze affectionately any hand she happened to be clinging to. Furthermore, she was the simple kind who probably thought Jimmy held her hand because he wanted to.

On the day of the Thanksgiving Turkey Shoot, she came for the event with her family. Jimmy was there too, and so was his best friend, Big Shorty's boy. This was the Lippincotts' third Thanksgiving at Wide Ruins, and by this time any affair held at the trading post was well attended. Indians from all over the desert came to the Turkey Shoot. The little Belai girl was all dressed up in stockings that spiraled around her skinny legs, and in a new gingham dress which somehow on her small frame hung like a curtain at a barn show. She spied Jimmy and made for him happily, and before he could disappear had her warm little hand tucked wartily into his.

There came a start of anguish to Jimmy's face, and the Shorty boy whooped for joy. The anguish was short-lived. Jimmy yanked free his hand and pointed furiously at his friend. That is the way all Navaho fights start, by somebody pointing at someone. The Shorty boy promptly retaliated with a shrill and vituperative yell of "Coyote!"—a deadly insult, and with various embellishments the worst thing a Navaho can be called. Whereupon they fell to pummeling each other for all they were worth, in front of the store doorway. The little Belai girl peeked out from behind her mother's skirts, and the crowd, which had set out to spend an afternoon in diversion anyway, gathered around at this unexpected aside.

Usually Jimmy could take care of himself fairly well in his fights. A few days before he had even trounced the school bully. The latter was the biggest boy in the room, naturally, since it had taken him a good many years to get that far. For a long time Jimmy managed to keep a discreet distance be-

tween himself and the heckler, but something had come up
in the trading-post yard after school, and before Jimmy could
slither away, the onlookers had delightedly blocked the two
in. Jimmy had been so honestly frightened he'd started trem-
bling all over, and tears had started in his eyes. And then,
suddenly crazed by his fears, he'd jumped the bully and was
wildly all over him. The other was bigger and stronger than
Jimmy, but he couldn't combat that inward ferocity. But that
victory had come largely through fear, and not having that
spur in the present scuffle with his friend, Jimmy was not
coming off so well.

Big Shorty's boy got him down and sat on him—sitting on
his hands. With his fists thus out of it, there came a pause.
Evidently, from what happened next, there went through
Jimmy's mind some thought of perhaps Superman, or Terry,
or Pop Eye, or maybe Joe Palooka. It was impossible to know
the way of that mind, since the little boy still never said anything to his young white friends beyond a yes and no. But
there came gleanings, now and then, of a deliciously surpris-
ing variety of things stowed away under that shock of unruly
black hair.

Jimmy's pony, for instance, he called Sliver. This puzzled
Sallie until one day the source became clear—with a slight
change in pronunciation. She saw him tearing recklessly down
the road on it yelling, "Heigho, Sliver!"

So if Jimmy knew the Lone Ranger programs, from the
Lippincotts' radio, he probably also knew the other various
heroes of the air and tabloids who seem destined to go through
life throwing around people twice their own weight. And
some such thought for the Shorty boy must have crossed his
mind, for he tried it. What happened, of course, was sad.
Jimmy got his head banged on the low heavy wooden doorstep.

Sallie gathered him up off his head and led him encouragingly into the house—with Jimmy as always following at about ten paces, but following, and this time sobbing stoically. Sallie washed him off and made an ice pack for the bump that was coming, and put him on the floor in the library with a pillow, and tried to console him by telling him that everybody got licked now and then—that nobody could win all the time. As usual he made no verbal reply to anything she was saying, but by the fury his sobbing had taken on now, his defeat was merely building up to fighting fuel. She left him, a little helplessly, with the general impression that as soon as he got his wind, he was going back and choke his friend Shorty, and if that Belai girl took hold of his hand again he'd take it and wring her arm off along with it.

The Turkey Shoot, by that time, was getting under way. Bill had the target put up beyond the sheep corral on the other side of the road, and the Indians were gathered around, to watch or shoot. Although it was late November the Arizona sun was deep in everything that day, in the bones and in the color that was everywhere.

Indian women and children were sitting like bright sage clumps up on the hillside, and the rifle barrels of the guns the men had slung across their backs were shining. A few onlookers were leaning against the corral fence. A few stayed in the store yard. Only one man there had on a white shirt, and his black hair fell long and loose against it, as he leaned against the white store wall. An Indian woman in a crimson skirt with a red and green striped shawl was bent over a sack of something she had put down on the ground; there was a brown horse patiently beside her, and behind them both a brown hill against a blue sky. At the crest of the hill sat an Indian in a red shirt and tan sombrero, on a black and white horse. Slowly down the road, on foot, came two Indian women, one with a baby—the mother and her baby both were looking out from the same shawl. Everything there was pattern. Nothing natural in that country seemed able to make a mistake where line and color were concerned.

The old medicine man was there, wearing a striped blanket today, which he wrapped around him. As usual he stood with his arms folded staring nobly off into space. He stood listening to the crack and whine of bullets, with the sound trailing off behind a hill and dying. His bronzed face was hawklike and thoughtful. He had had his share of white scalps in his time, and been captured, and come back.

If it all was colorful, the Lippincotts' handy man was positively resplendent. Joe was walking around with an important frown of concentration on his face, with never a glance at anyone, and very conscious of the new shirt he had bought for the occasion. It was American Beauty up one side, and lavender up the other, with the sleeves divided between orange and blue. Bill had tried to argue him out of buying it.

"Look at Hasteen Belai," he had urged—the hand-holding little girl's father who was, comparatively speaking, a man of substance. "He doesn't spend his money foolishly like you, and he always has ten or fifteen dollars in his pocket."

"Yes," smirked Joe, "but he no have fine shirt like me." Not only did Joe have a fine shirt, but he had replaced its ordinary buttons with a row of handsome silver ones.

"Joe Toddy!" He was being summoned. "Take your shot."

Up he strutted, with a flash of happy teeth at this prominence. Joe squatted, and squirmed, and took as much pains and time getting into position as a golfer does to tee off. Then he took a long aim and missed.

Wisecracks flew back and forth—mostly in Navaho, with now and then one in English. "Give him a rock and I think he can make it." "That's the right idea, but the wrong direction."

Those used to shooting with bow and arrows were allowed

to take their shots sitting or prone. Bullets cracked carelessly around in any direction as the shooters practiced, and when someone shot an extra big gun, everyone laughed at the bigness of the noise.

There was a horse race on the side—a good two hours was spent making up the bets, with the race itself lasting about three seconds, and the bets tossed down on a blanket. It was a bad day for Joe. Not only had his aim missed for the turkey, but he lost all his silver buttons on the horse race, and at the end was going around with his fine shirt held together by safety pins. Navahos are inveterate gamblers, and usually take their losses with an indifference which equals their laughter when the gains are raked in. But Joe had that glum look he always got after he realized he'd spent too much money. And now he'd have to have horse for his Thanksgiving dinner instead of turkey. He stood looking banefully at the winded animal who had let him down, as though if he had to have "hawrse" he'd just as leave have that one.

The four prize turkeys that had been waiting in the store garage were uncrated and given to the winners and one turkey got away, with Indians after it—picking up its feathers to give to the medicine man to use in his next sing. By the time the Thanksgiving Turkey Shoot was over, shadows were lying long in the west.

The turkeys for the first Thanksgiving were shot down and brought to the feast by the owners of the country, the Indians, as welcome to the white newcomers on the continent. Now, some several hundred years later, the turkeys belonged to the white people, although the Indians still were allowed to shoot for them.

Sometime in the affair Jimmy had come out from the house and into the crowd, and when it was over he was standing with his friend Shorty. But there was abstraction about him, a distance about him. He'd forgotten about the quarrel with Shorty, and with the little Belai girl. The Belai girl was standing off to the side, a lollipop in her mouth, and looking at him at a loss. A faint harassment was beginning to show about her, but back in, as though it were something that had happened to her before she was born, which would never quite let her catch up, nor quite let her know that either.

Jimmy had forgotten both the Belai girl and his friend Shorty in a spectacle bigger than any quarrel among them, although they all were of it.

He left them and crossed the road, as though he were remembering something—something which would stay the one real thing in all the intricate webbing and spreading of his life—some involuntary compulsion to record his impressions: no matter of desire or volition, yet bigger than personal obligation and obstacle; bigger than he was, using all of him there was to use.

He went into the room at the back of the store that was his, and did the first painting since summer. He painted a big, tired turkey, standing on a red, white, and blue line. It was not a particularly good picture, in itself. But it had his own ways in it. Jimmy had come back, the surer for his traveling.

CHAPTER

9

THE Thanksgiving Turkey Shoot was over and Joe, back to his limp black shirt again, had grown resigned to his gambling losses. He had not had turkey for Thanksgiving, it is true, due to his aim being poor, but he had compensated for that by having horse for dinner. "Nize," he had commented vaguely, of his Thanksgiving horse dinner. Now he was going around muttering "May Clizmus"—getting in practice.

It was coming on toward Sallie's and Bill's third Christmas at Wide Ruins, and they found the Indians around them slightly confused by the approaching season. They knew it was the time the white people celebrated the birth of Jesus— and they knew all about Jesus. The Navahos have been hearing about Jesus ever since Benavides began trying to convert them, by means of the Spanish sword, in 1629. Later the Franciscan Fathers built the mission at St. Michael's and settled down to a gentler but equally persistent attempt, along with the Presbyterians who entered the field at Ganado.

And up to a point, the Navahos around Wide Ruins humor both groups. At appointed times the Catholics come around to the trading post and hand out medals which the Indians are pleased to have and which they promptly sew on their blouses and moccasins as buttons. Then the next week they are Presbyterians, so they can get the pretty bright Bible pictures to hang on their hogan walls.

Joe himself had a spell of being a Presbyterian. The time Sallie and Bill took their handy man with them to Colorado Springs to buy horses, they also took him to an ice-skating carnival, and Joe thought all the beautiful girls skimming blindingly around over the ice with their dazzling smiles and their spangly short skirts were the angels the Presbyterians always were talking about, and he came home an enthusiastic convert. However, at his first real feeling of need, he turned instinctively to the old medicine man.

The missionaries will not get their inning until the white culture shows itself to be the stronger of the two, and that of the Navahos breaks under its pressure—which it hasn't done so far. But when that does break, its sociological history will be that of complete demoralization for a while.

There is a little church at San Ildefonso, however, which was built at the time of the Spanish conquistadores, and which is a fine example of present-day tolerance on both sides. Just before the winter Buffalo Dance which Sallie and Bill attended once, a service is held there in the dawn. It is a very impressive service, with the old church lighted only by candles stuck in tin holders on the thick mud walls, and the priest in his ornate robes chanting in Latin while a wildly colorful Indian congregation kneels on the packed earth floor. Then every few minutes two men at the back of the church shoot off rifles. The idea is to keep the evil spirits away, but if Sallie had known about the custom beforehand, it would have kept her away too. They shoot just one shot at a time, and the guns are so old they have to be taken almost apart and put together again in the process of reloading. The pause for this is just long enough to lull visitors into a false sense of security, when wham!—a gun goes off again. The congregation never seems to notice, and the priest drones on without looking up. But the uninitiated come out from church completely unnerved.

The Catholic tolerance of the service is something which is thought about afterward.

The Navahos in general feel tenderly and personally about the idea of Jesus. Jesus was a shepherd, and so are they. The confusion that Sallie and Bill discovered in their minds still, was the matter of his exact birthday.

On this particular day a delegation of troubled Navahos came into the store to ask the young white people about it. Each year, as long as the Lippincotts had been there, the Franciscan monks had made the trip across the desert from St. Michael's and handed out presents, but since roads are unpredictable at that time of year, they had come whenever they could get there. In like manner, the Presbyterians would make the trek from Ganado to hold a Christmas ceremony after the Presbyterian custom. Then, on the last day of school, the teachers would hold a celebration. The traders, being on the grounds, waited until Christmas morning itself to hand out stockings from the store. The whole thing was throwing the Indians into complete turmoil. Just how many Jesuses got born every year?

But if they were bewildered by the details of the calendar, they were very clear, instinctively so, in the general concept— that of the world's rebirth of hope through its new generations.

The Navahos are racially good to children—their own, and all children. Indeed they so pity people who have no children that often they will generously present the so deprived with one of their own. This is a practice that makes up one of the several reasons why census takers are not happy in their work in that part of the country, but in itself the motive springs pure. And they will take a waif under their wing as though it were a privilege.

Thus it was that on Sallie's and Bill's first Christmas at Wide Ruins, when Little Woman came to bring them a present of a sack of colored ears of corn, she had a toddler happily in tow. The child could not have been hers, even by a minor miracle, for Little Woman was many times over the winters old that even the Biblically remarkable Sarah had been. Little Woman attempted no explanation of the child, nor doubtless did the necessity of an explanation occur to her. And Joe said airily, when later they asked if he knew, "Oh, he's just a mifflin"—or so it sounded. Joe might have been taking a try at "orphlan"—it was hard to tell, Joe sliffed and slurred his English so. But at any rate, from that moment on the child whom Little Woman had always with her was known matter-of-factly around the trading post as the Mifflin.

The Mifflin that first Christmas morning appeared at the snowy front door of the house with nothing but rags on his feet. Bill picked him up and carried him inside. And while Sallie sat on the hearth cutting the rags from his feet, Bill went in the store to outfit him, and the three of them then had a great time putting his new things on him—Little Woman standing by toothless and beatific. The two stayed for dinner—Little Woman had hers cross-legged on the hearth, and there wasn't a crumb left. But the Mifflin was too excited to eat. He kept walking around proudly, taking high steps and stopping at each step to stoop down and examine his new boots.

That was the Christmas Sallie introduced the Navaho children to the thrill of zinging downhill on a sled and ending up with their faces in the snow. But in this the older Navahos soon had the children crowded off the sled track. Such tittering and giggling! The men took their courage in their hands and went down belly floppers as Sallie showed them, but the women insisted on keeping to their dignity and sitting upright. Their big full skirts acted like snowplows.

Now Christmas was coming again. Already some of the Navahos had a Christmas fund. The fund was an innovation with this year, and they'd thought it up themselves. Sallie and Bill were rather baffled, but they went along in it. They kept the jar for it in the store, and kept a list of the people who were contributing because they had been instructed to give the ultimate kitty to the schoolteacher, who was to buy presents for the ones on the list. In some respects the Navaho culture grows not so differently from the ways the white culture has fallen into. The kitty had been in operation for several weeks, and to date had five pennies in it. Sallie and Bill decided the contributors probably figured the traders would add something—and they probably would.

Christmas was coming and already big Texas Mary out in the kitchen was making ponderous memorandums to be taken along to Gallup the next time anybody went in for supplies— for popcorn to make popcorn balls, and spices and new cutters for the innumerable gingerbread men and animals and sugar-sparkled stars, and for nuts to roast; sugar for the fudge squares; oranges and apples to fill up the toes of the stockings which would be handed out Christmas morning—to eager big children trying not to look it, and to ones so little their mothers would come bringing them in their arms.

> Ahwae, ahwae, safe in my arms,
> Ahwae, ahwae, my little one—

The brown-skinned mothers would croon to their ahwae, their babies, as they stood holding them in their arms, waiting.

> Out of the darkness into the light
> Came ahwae, ahwae, my little one

goes the Navaho song.

And in the irregular mails coming in from the outside world excitingly were beginning to arrive distinctive packages with their cool surface labels slightly battered by the trip but still holding—Marshall Field, Saks, Abercrombie & Fitch, I. Magnin. . . . And going out excitingly from the post by truck or by an Indian on horseback were packages equally distinctive, but different. A package from the Wide Ruins trading post might have anything in it—from turquoise boxes and silver pieces beaten out of a big round dollar with just enough alloy in the silver to mellow it; or maybe it would be a bundle of the sweet little brown pinion nuts, tied in a square of the bright red cloth which the Indian squaws buy for their full skirts. One recipient of a very large and heavy package, which arrived parcel post, opened it startledly to find four logs—because Sallie had remembered how she'd liked the particular illusiveness of juniper and pinion wood burning together, when she'd been at Wide Ruins.

Packages were going and coming, and so were Christmas cards. The latter proved a field day for Jimmy. As they came in, Sallie passed them on to him, knowing the child's delight in papers of different textures and colors, and his resourcefulness with them. Jimmy did astonishing things with the Lippincott friends' greetings to them. On the red side of one card he abstractedly experimented with a little black porcupine looking sleepy. Then in the way one idea linked to another in his mind, he took the next red one that came along, which was duller but still warm, and made a campfire scene—merely by letting the already present warm color of the paper suggest the fire and adding white flame and black shadows. The following year, this painting was pointed out particularly in the art column of the *San Diego Tribune Sun*, after a showing of his work at the Art Center at La Jolla. The art column that day was headed with the quotation, "Life is full of meaning and purpose—so full of beauty."

"It is finished in beauty"—that is the way all Navaho chants and prayers end.

Beauty was easy to think about in places like the Wide Ruins valley. It was so right at hand, with long moments of it untrammeled by people. For a little while, after the delegation of Indians had left the store, there was nothing of people anywhere outside in the trading-post yard. Just sun and space and quiet. There was not a sound, except the wind in the cottonwoods. The young white cottonwood by the road waved and shone, and the old one on the other side of the patio wall, rising above it, had the shy dignity of quiet things, and beyond through its plain branches was the wider quiet of the sky. There was a simple strongness to moments like that—a purity to their heartsease.

It was almost Christmas, and all the brown hills were looking warm, almost with a misty look. The quiet winter hills had a promise of fertility.

And then, into the quiet, way off somewhere, came faintly on the high clear air the sound of a shepherd singing to his flock—singing the owl song that keeps them safe. Perhaps the shepherds on the brown hills in the time of Jesus had sung some such song, too. And Jimmy, as his conception of Christmas that year, painted on gray-night paper a white mother sheep, hovering with a nice look in her eye over her two little ewe lambs, both nearly all black.

CHAPTER

10

IT WAS spring again. The Navahos were saying with satisfaction, "Da nahazli!"—meaning "Spring returned again!" The Navaho term for it has a triumphant surge.

It was spring, and Jimmy would ride his pony past the trading post in the mornings before school and in the evenings, as though the time of year and having a pony of his own in it let him own the world. He still was too shy to ride with Sallie and Bill, although they frequently invited him. But afterward he would ride their horses up to the corral for them, and do it with such pride.

Horses, like sheep, are a vital part of the Navaho racial structure. Ever since the days when the Spaniards first invaded the Southwest, riding gloriously in on their steeds in the name of Philip, the Navahos have had horses. The first ones they took directly from Philip's men, and the ensuing generations got them from the ones the Spaniards left in the hills to go wild and breed. These wild horses were fighters. Left to their own resources, they had to fight for very existence against wolves and panthers—and they fought among themselves. The stallions fought for their mates, and for herd supremacy. The ruler of a herd came to his position by might. It was a life of kicking, biting, blood, and recklessness they lived among themselves.

There are thousands of these mustangs still in the Arizona hills, and sometimes they can be seen in headlong flight. It is not the sleek thundering of western romances, however. After generations of fighting off animals as hungry as they, and fighting among themselves, they are now a light-bodied, torn-coated, scraggy lot. But in the winter, when the mountain grasses fail and some of them venture down into the valleys, the sight of half a dozen of them scrambling up over the rocks of the wash just beyond Wide Ruins still has a grace and a power to it.

The Navahos hunt these horses eagerly, to sell for a few dollars to buy silk shirts and silver; or if mutton is scarce and they need food, they make a stew of them. But mostly they are caught and tamed for mounts. The more horses a Navaho has, the greater his standing in the community. Nevertheless, although the possession of horses makes the world know how important a man is, as a rule, once they get that possession, the Navahos are very indifferent to the needs of their horses. They feed their animals sparingly—generally turning them loose to browse where they can, after the day's use. Nor do they take care of them when they are sick or get hurt. And a curry comb is never thought of.

But Jimmy was good to the pony he called Sliver, and Sliver was his chief pleasure. It was only a dun-colored little animal with stripes around its legs, of the wild variety—only it wasn't very wild, except in the little boy's loyal imagination. Jimmy would squat on his heels and study the lines of the pony, or drift his fingers down the arch of its stubby mane, as though Sliver were of a famous line, and bred for swiftness. He groomed the pony and kept it as shining as he could, considering what he had to work with. And the pony's shoulders would ripple with pleasure under the sure, confident little hand. Jimmy had a way with horses, and when the boy would lay a hand on Sliver's back and jump on, whatever fleetness the pony had, it mustered.

Joe had a horse, too, in which he was very interested, and

which he called Dotse. "Dotse good hawrse," Joe would stoutly maintain of Dotse's trustworthiness to stand without tethering, while at that very moment Dotse was heading for the wash as fast as her scrubby legs would take her. The horses of the hills, although they stampede in terror at the first approach of man, once they are caught and tamed usually grow very fond of human beings. Dotse had a positive obsession on the subject. Dotse just loved people. So at every opportunity she would head for the wash, knowing somebody would come get her out, because she never failed to get befuddled in midstream, and someone had to guide her to shore. Then she would clamber out and come up close to her rescuer and shake like a dog. By experience she came to know that people moved away if they saw her coming, so she would make her approach slyly, step at a time, until she managed to get right beside them, or behind them. Then she would lean against them, getting heavier and heavier.

Dotse was a character, but Joe's chief interest in her was that the visitors who rode her—as a last resort if the other horses were taken—would give him a quarter for Dotse's hire. That had been Joe's idea, and he had been very disappointed when it hadn't worked at its initial venture.

The very first visitor to Wide Ruins, indeed while Wide Ruins was only a dream that was not at all certain yet, was a man with more outward dignity and inward humor and kindness than usually is found. A man of quiet tolerance—but he drew the line at Dotse. Dotse in Navaho means "maybe." Joe shuffled gloomily around for several days, but at the end of that first stay, the visitor shook hands with him, and that brightened him. The visitor had left a tip in the handy man's hand for his general services, whereupon ever after Joe beamingly and devotedly called him the Man Who Shakes Hands with Money.

Another of the early visitors at Wide Ruins had also among

her experiences there one which included a brush with a horse. Hers came during a rodeo at a neighboring trading post. This particular guest was the kind who was quite certain one would no more travel without evening clothes than one would without a toothbrush, and they all started regally for the rodeo in her Packard. She had traveled widely, but a back-in desert was new to her, and since she was there, she intended to see it. When they came to a turn in the road which interested her, she picked up the speaking tube and gave the chauffeur the order. Sallie tried to explain that a car that heavy wouldn't get three feet through the particular sandiness of the road. Objections were waved aside. The chauffeur moved up nearer the edge of the seat, gripped the wheel, made the turn—and the car promptly bedded itself down to the hub.

Fortunately they still were near enough Wide Ruins for help to be assembled, and while the visitor sat in the back seat calmly reading a magazine, Indians shoveled and sweated, and concocted purchase. When the right moment came, the chauffeur got in and started the ticklish application of power, and slowly, while the workers stood by hopefully, leaning exhaustedly on their shovels, the wheels began to grind their way out. Feeling motion in the car, the visitor looked up from her reading, smiled pleasantly, took a sheaf of bills from her bag and leaned forward and tapped the chauffeur on the shoulder.

"Pay the men."

"But, madame!"

"Pay the men—"

The chauffeur slumped, with a licked motion, released the gas to pay the men, and the car sagged back in the hole.

However, Navaho local rodeos are disorganized affairs, with few events scheduled beforehand, and even those coming off in quite different order from that announced on the program.

So that even after three more hours of shoveling, they still got there in time for the main feature—that of roping a wild horse.

Navahos are surprisingly inept with a rope, although they always try it. Jimmy was trying his hand at it. At first he had practiced on things that wouldn't move—like the hitching post in the trading-post yard. Then he practiced on his father's horse Dotse—until Dotse began running and hiding behind a sage bush every time she saw him. He practiced on other people's horses, but he never bothered Sliver with it.

The Lippincotts and their guest found seats on a grandstand which was as makeshift as everything else about the rodeo, with nothing but trust between the spectators and the activities in the field. Their guest sat erect, looking on pleasantly, when suddenly—with a yell of warning as announcement—a wild stallion, crazed by fear and the spurring it had been taking to put zest into the event, plunged from one of the chutes into the arena. It wheeled from under the rope hurled ineffectively at it, and charged, stampeding for the barrier straight in front of it—the grandstand—obviously blindly bent on hurtling its way to freedom regardless of obstacles. The two young people leaped to their feet in horror. They threw themselves protectively in front of their guest, and then, in that blankness of mind in which, contrary to all fiction, one awaits the end, they closed their eyes. When they opened them again, the terrorized animal had skidded on past and was recklessly breaking through a barbed-wire fence, well to the right of the grandstand. Limply they turned to their guest. She was still looking on, smiling pleasantly, quite undisturbed and surprised that they should be. A wild horse would not attack her. It wouldn't dare.

To their real astonishment, she became one of Wide Ruins' approvers. She went so far in her concession to the democracy of the idea as to take part in the social hour after a squaw dance which the Indians held one night in the trading-post yard.

She looked on with interest, and after the dance was over stood by the campfire roasting marshmallows, and handing them graciously to the slightly mystified old medicine man.

The fame of Wide Ruins as a place of adventure grew so broad that the Lippincotts had to put up two guest houses. One they called The Little House, and the other they built of red cedar posts, in the manner of a Navaho hogan, with ancient grinding stones as steps leading up to it.

Guests came from all parts of the country, and sometimes disconcertingly. One morning the Lippincotts looked out the window to see two people they had never seen before in their lives, taking a great many bags out of the car in a very business-like manner. The newcomers made themselves comfortably at home all day before they realized that Wide Ruins was not, as they had been led to suppose from roundabout accounts of it, a dude ranch. In their great embarrassment, they tried putting in the time until they could decently leave in the morning, by walking out over the desert. It did not add to their composure that a bat got into The Little House that night, and in trying to drive it out the man threw his wife's coat at it, which had some pretty stones she'd picked up in the desert in its pockets, so that the coat crashed on out through the window. After a few more such experiences, misadventure began to be accepted as part of the adventure, so that it turned out to be adventure capital A, and one of the better visits, on both sides.

The next time an unannounced guest arrived at their doorstep, bag in hand, it was because a mutual friend had talked to him enthusiastically about the peace and quiet of Wide Ruins —the heart balm and body ease of it—and the other had said wishfully, being tired, "I'd like to go some place like that."

"Go ahead," his friend had urged generously. "It'll be all right. I'll write Sallie and Bill you're coming." Only he had forgotten to write.

The mutual friend did write, however, in the case of the two girls from England. They were Wrens who had come directly from England to Washington, and they spent their first leave at Wide Ruins. Having seen nothing more of America than their months in Washington, they took a plane West, came to the middle of a desert, and could well understand what they always had heard about America—that it still had Indians. The place was full of them!

From there on, the girls from England learned about the great West in little ways—the gray and white flash of the little juncos as they rode through the sage; the scream of the pinion jay; the feel of the horses' hooves sinking deep into the red sand. There was the leisure of winding miles up a canyon with its steep sides green, sometimes rocky, with once an eagle's nest high in the branching of a twin yellow pine; stopping at a rocky fork to watch the water swirling below; wandering back through pinion woods, past a tiny corral for lambs born far from home—and into the clear again, with its wide space. Visiting Wide Ruins was like stepping outside the world for a while, and that was a becalming place to be right then.

Easterners who came found out that all western horses neck rein, and that you don't post—the western saddle was built for practical purposes; you couldn't post while you roped a steer. It was the same with chaps—they weren't worn to be fancy; they were lifesavers riding through the gnarly sage. Also the metal tips on boots—a broken sage branch could break off all your toes without that protection, and the high heel of the western boot was to dig into the ground so the horse or steer wouldn't drag you. The sombrero was designed for the functional purpose of keeping you from being slapped off your seat by the switching of low branches; also to keep the rain from going down your neck. The colored silk handkerchief knotted so picturesquely at the throat was not just for decoration—it kept the wind off the back of your neck, and when it was cold you could wrap it around your middle under your shirt to help keep you warm; you could weigh it down with sand or a rock and tether your horse, or you could put coffee in it and boil it.

There was the brisk old lady who came, and went traipsing over the country with a box of raisins and a chocolate bar. She had never ridden except side saddle, and that years ago, but she stayed astride four hours at a time at Wide Ruins.

There was the old couple who stopped one night, with a horse and wagon, on their way to look for gold. All kind of lost treasure still is in the West, with as many people hunting it as before. There still are almost-findings of the Seven Cities of Cibola, and Cortez' mine with the famous iron door where the Spaniards stored their gold and silver and precious stones back in the sixteenth century, and which people continue losing their lives and their fortunes trying to find. There were stories of people actually finding gold, and then not being able to find their way back to it.

And the same hope and credulity which had stampeded the country in '49, brought the two old people to Wide Ruins, on their way. They had a faded diary with them, which after a few hours they decided to show to Bill, to see if he could help them. It was the diary of a wagon train coming across the desert. The writer had gone aside to hunt, up a narrow box canyon, at the top of which he had come to a sharp turn which a horse could make but a wagon couldn't. Here the name of a pine was mentioned which Bill happened to know grew only at 5000 feet above sea level—so the anxious old people found that much confirmation in their search. Also the diary went on to say that looking west from that point there was a broad plateau. But it was a whole country of broad plateau they were in, varied by countless buttes and mesas and gorges and washes.

Bill could only give them an estimate of where that particular span might lie. But at the turn of the canyon which overlooked it, the writer had found some strange rocks which he had picked up and taken on to California, where they were assayed and found to be seventy per cent gold. All the people in the wagon train, then, had tried to find their way back to the place, but they couldn't get through the Indians. They were wiped out. Now the diary was in the hands of the writer's great-nephew—hands, as he took it again, which trembled at treasure being that much nearer.

There was supposed to be gold right around Wide Ruins. Two Mexicans had come in once and found a rock float of a soft grayish white cast and with gold showing plainly in it. They dug some of it out with their knives and hands, and put it in their bandannas—made a cairn to mark the spot, and rode back into Gallup. But on the way one of them killed the other, then in Gallup he got to drinking and talked and told—and got killed himself. But nobody was ever able to find that float again. Loukaichukai said he knew where it was. But he wouldn't tell anybody. He said the gold wouldn't do the Indians any good, and if he told the white people they'd bring in machines and take it out. He said it was best to let it stay where it was.

Sallie and Bill never heard whether the old couple found the gold they were looking for. The two young people stood together in the trading-post yard watching the horse pull the wagon slowly up over the hill, the backs of the old people bent a little, as they looked ahead down the road.

Then there was their friend the professor whose main interest in the equestrian aspect of Wide Ruins turned toward sponsoring the first eastern exhibit of Jimmy's paintings. Horses always had figured largely in the little boy's paintings. From that first day Sallie and Bill had found him, the drawing of horses had been in the growth of his work. He had painted a belligerent mouse-colored little horse, with a black mane like a day's beard, and with its black feet braced stubbornly, against pale-green construction paper. Later on, as he began experimenting with different mediums, he did a brush-line painting like an etching. It was of a mare with her colt close beside her— the colt so echoed in the lines of the mare it was not seen for itself at first. He did a big, patient, pink plow horse. He painted two brown mules standing side by side but facing in opposite directions so that although their bodies seemed one, they were looking different ways.

Horses played a great part in the life at Wide Ruins, and most people who had any association with the place enjoyed that aspect of it especially. But not everyone. Not everyone, in fact, enjoyed Wide Ruins. Some people were very unhappy there.

One of the latter was an old school friend who couldn't believe the Lippincotts had turned Indian traders, and on his way to the Coast he stopped off to see for himself. He had never driven off a highway, and that eighteen miles of narrow sand road in from Chambers got him off to a bad start. However, Bill assured him that the fall rains were over—it was late November—and the roads should be passable for some time yet. He had been there about half an hour when one of those rains which were supposed to be over suddenly hit. Afterward they all went to look at his road, but there wasn't any. It had washed away. Just the bridge—as usual, after such rains, hanging in mid air, with nothing going to it or from it.

He had intended to stop only for a few hours, but since he couldn't possibly leave before morning, he agreed to see something of the country by horseback.

"Get 'em oop da hawrses now?" asked Joe.

"And put the saddles on Creed and Pantywaist and Shucks,"

"The colt was so echoed in the lines of the mare, it was not seen for itself at first."

Bill told him explicitly, seeing the light of a quarter in the handy man's survey of the guest.

Shucks was a Kentucky Thoroughbred, and Creed and Pantywaist the two Palominos they had bought in Colorado Springs. Creed was stronger than most Palominos. In fact he once had bucked a snowstorm for four days in the rescue of an exploring party. Even the amateur riders felt sureness and confidence in Creed, as though they could depend upon him to carry them through. The mare Pantywaist was smaller, with Arab in her— it showed in her face and throat. Pantywaist was passionately devoted to Creed, and if Creed got out of her sight on a long stretch, she would go racing after him sobbing frenziedly until she came up with him again, and then she was inclined toward the sideways dancing idea. Dependability was not Pantywaist's strong point. But compared to Joe's horse Dotse, she was a Gibraltar.

Joe, at the saddling order shutting Dotse out, grew stubborn. "He ride my hawrse, Dotse," he insisted brightly.

"What's Dotse?"

"Dotse's an Indian horse. You don't want to ride Dotse."

On the contrary, he did. Since he was stuck in the wilds anyway, he might as well go the whole way, and at least get dinner-table conversation out of it. The Lippincotts did what they could to co-operate.

They took him on the ride to the old deer corral. They pounded up the trail from the post, Creed leading and Pantywaist close on his tail, with Dotse bringing up in the rear. They went plowing through tough sage, plunged into unexpected little washes created by the rain. It was a long way to the deer corral, ducking under murderous pinion branches, scrambling up over rocks. Once, half-way up the mountain, a boulder rose in the trail. The two front horses reared, wheeled, and went around it. But Dotse, who had been panting and sweating and straining to keep up anyway, came to a dead stop and looked at it as though that were the last straw. Her rider gave a dig with his spurs, and Dotse took one reluctant step forward. He kept at her. Finally, with a great sigh, Dotse just dove at the rock, sprawling all over it—the rider sprawling too.

The deer corral, when they at last got to it, was a brush-fenced enclosure up on the side of the mountain. It was a relic of the days when the Navahos hunted down their meat. They would drive the deer into the corral, and then shoot the trapped animals. The guest looked at the corral, and then at Dotse, thoughtfully.

They went on to the top of the mountain, and down the other side, through wet tangles and slippery growth and over so many rocks they dismounted and led the horses. Dotse was not used to being led. The going was precarious enough anyway, but Dotse would get up close to the guest and give him a nudge, sending him flat. He'd get up and smack her face. Then Dotse would sulk and wouldn't budge. Finally he turned the animal loose and audibly hoped the lions and coyotes would get her.

Dotse just stood still where she was, watching the others zigzagging their way down through the rough brush. Looking back, they could see her white-blazed face turning as they turned, like someone watching a tennis match. Then when she lost them, she grew frantic and came plunging straight down to where they were—with the guest having to dodge like a bull-fighter to get out of her way. Dotse was tired when she stopped. She took two mouthfuls of grass, then with the grass sticking out of her mouth like a mustache, she fell fast asleep, leaning against the visitor heavily.

He got up late the next morning, and came stiffly into the living room where Sallie was reading the *Gallup Gazette* by the fire. It had grown colder in the night.

"How cold does it have to get before that damned road will harden up enough to travel?"

"Oh, about thirty."

He went over and opened the top half of the outside door and looked at the thermometer on the porch wall.

"Forty," he reported glumly.

"Feels about like forty," agreed Sallie. "What would you like for breakfast?—and he'll have it here, Bess."

Bess, who was flicking a dust cloth around the living room, looked up brightly.

"Oh, anything—toast—" he told her, impatiently.

"Want me to read you the *Gallup Gazette*?" asked Sallie, when Bess had departed kitchenward.

"No."

She read it anyway. "'The Garcia Brothers, leading cowmen of French Fence, were in Gallup yesterday for dental work.'"

"How the devil did they get there, by tank?"

"This is last week's paper," she explained. "But even then," she discovered, "traveling wasn't too good. 'Joe Akins and family, enroute to Gallup from Top of the World, broke a spring and had to be pulled into Gallup by Chester Burt who happened along with a load of beans on his truck.'"

The guest withheld comment.

"'Do your Christmas shopping in Gallup.'"

"By God, I might at that!"

"Only you couldn't get there."

He slung a log at the fire. Sallie looked up questioningly.

"Maybe you'd like to go into business? Here's an 'A-1 filling station. Owner going good. Ideal business for live wire. Get details.'"

He strode over to the door and looked at the thermometer again. "Still forty. Does this thing ever stick?"

"Not that I know of."

The kitchen door was kicked open, and Bess came briskly in with a breakfast tray. He slumped down to the davenport, and then straightened and stared at the tray on the coffee table in front of him. There was one small plate on it, and set squarely in the middle of the plate, a piece of toast. He looked at Bess. The Navaho girl looked back. That's what the gentleman had asked for, and that's what he got.

"Your infatuation for this place," he told Sallie, when she had sent Bess back for bacon and eggs, "infuriates me. What in hell is there about it for you to like?"

"Oh, I don't know—the *Gallup Gazette* kind of fascinates me, I guess. 'The Clawson boys,' she went on to report, 'who ride past the reservoir, say that the water at that point on the road is now knee deep to a saddle horse.' "

The guest regarded her bitterly.

That was in November. Now it was spring again and the soft white cotton bits on the cottonwoods which gave the trees their name were like the last snow of the year against the blue sky. The horses lost their shaggy winter look, and Jimmy was riding recklessly past the post yelling, "Heigho, Sliver!"

Then all at once they realized that for several days they had not seen Jimmy riding past. They had not seen the little boy at all. He did not come to his studio every day, it was true—he came only when he wanted to. But they usually saw him around. They asked Joe what had happened to Jimmy lately, and the Navaho looked at them strangely, with something of fear in the look.

He told them, slowly, uncertainly, that something had got the matter with Sliver, and the pony had wandered off into the desert—that Jimmy had gone out to find it. He said Jimmy hunted for his pony three days, and when he found it, it was dead—and he had buried it. That was why Joe was looking at the young white people strangely.

Navahos are bound by countless prohibitive superstitions which spring from fear. Chindee—taboo. But of all things chindee, the fear of the dead is the most powerfully rooted, the most unbreakable one. Not far from the trading post, under a pile of rock, was a saddle lying only half hidden from the view of the most casual passer-by. It evidently had been there for years, for the leather was rotting away. None of the Navahos around Wide Ruins would have touched that saddle for the world, for fear of their very lives. It belonged to the dead, buried with it further in under the rock. And nobody touches the dead, or anything belonging to the dead.

The very hogans where someone has died are either burned or at once deserted and never entered again. When it seems likely someone in a hogan is going to die, that one is lifted outside, to meet the end of days alone.

The power of the fear of death is stronger even than the love of a mother for her child. A little boy was taken very ill in a family in the Wide Ruins community, and the mother had the medicine man come and give sing after sing for the child. They refused to take this child to the Ganado Hospital, as the white people wanted them to, because unfortunately another child they had taken there—too late—had died, and they would not trust the white people's way with this, their last son. But neither the medicine man's plea to the gods nor the medicinal herb waters that went with the ceremony seemed able to lift the child through a need beyond his own failing strength.

The day came when the mother bent over the boy and picked him up. And all that a mother can put into a last minute with her child, she put into the fierce tenderness with which she held him to her—and the child lifted his arms about her neck with, oddly, almost a protective gesture. No word was spoken between them. They both knew. She carried him outside the hogan, to a place a ways off, and put him on the ground, and turned, and without looking back left him.

Mercifully the usual four-day supply of bread and water which is left beside the dying was not needed. The mother did not go near to claim her dead. She took no part in the burial of the body, under rocks heaped upon it carefully—not touching the dead. Nor did she cry. But when she came again to the trading post it was as though her tears had been walled up within her, like some inward reservoir of depth, giving her a dignity, a certain coolness—an indifference to trivial things. She would go through her business at the store with that scornful indifference to the world of affairs which marks people who are acquainted with grief. And yet, she had left her child.

That was why Joe looked at the young white people strangely. Jimmy, who was as long-lined a Navaho as any on the reservation, had not been afraid of the dead, when his time of proving came. Or if he was afraid, something else had come to him that was stronger.

The little boy who had come to follow the ways of his young white friends in everything had seen them bury a Spaniel named Doc. They'd always made a great pet of Doc, although he was the rankest kind of thief. Doc consistently stole eggs from the store. He would come wandering out, with that innocent look Spaniels can get, and they'd pat him gently under his soft jowls—with Doc looking hurt at their mistrust. Then, when the egg would come out, Doc would be so surprised. They had buried their pet when it died, and so Jimmy, alone in the desert, had buried Sliver.

He did not come into the studio for a long time after Sliver died. Then one day he came in, hooked the heels of his yellow shoes over the rung of the chair, picked out a large piece of paper and painted a band of young horses in full flight—all the horses and all the youngness in the world were in it.

"All the horses and all the youngness in the world were in it."

CHAPTER

11

THE Lippincotts had not been in the trading-post business very long before they realized it was not one they could revolutionize overnight. Indeed, it might take some time before they could set up new policies, or even do much about squaring up the old ones. By early autumn of their third year they had gotten so far with changes as to quit sitting around on the counter half a day waiting for the Indians to make up their minds. They played darts instead.

They put up a dart board back of the dry goods counter and would stand at the other end of the store and pitch darts by the hour. Bill Cousins—the clerk whom they had hired to help them get on to the business, and who had proved such a valuable friend he still was with them—had such long arms and legs his listless lunges with the little feathered thing would take him half-way across the store, like a javelin thrower.

This was a sight which always astonished any chance traveler passing by and stopping in—three able-bodied white people pitching darts in the middle of the day, while a row of silent Indians on a bench looked on solemnly. Strangers entering an Indian trading post naturally expected to see Indian trading going on.

As a matter of actuality, Indian trading at its height was going on during those dart games. That was one of the first things the Lippincotts had found out in their Wide Ruins experience—that Indians can't be hurried. And there had been nothing in their three years since to change that observation. Easy, lazy ways—easy lazy days which had time in them for the weighing and laying in the balance of more than flour and sugar and wool, although there was plenty of that, too.

This morning, as soon as the store door was opened, there was Mrs. Beaver, on hand with some wool to sell. The big business in wool was almost over for the year, with the June clips. This June Navahos from a wider area than usual had brought their wool in to the Wide Ruins traders. Some of the wealthier herders had clips from flocks running into the hundreds, while the poorer ones perhaps had only one or two head. But anyone with sheep at all had clipped them and brought in their wool.

In July they had brought the sheep themselves to Wide Ruins, for dipping in the government vat there. Over a thousand Indians had come this year, and it had been quite an occasion— odorous as well as colorful. The strong smell of sheep fought with the antiseptic strength of the nicotine solution running through the vats on the other side of the road from the trading post. Navaho children usually take care of the family's sheep, but for this occasion the mothers helped. A mother in her dark blouse and brilliant skirt would lean over the vat to shove the protesting sheep through their bath by a prod of a shepherd's crook, and leaning beside her would be a little girl with her fat top tightly encased in dark velvet and her long skirts hiking up in the rear just like her mother's. This while the men talked sheep shop, and got up horse races. Now and then there would be a chicken pull—that ancient game of burying a live chicken to its neck in the sand, while Indians on horseback circled it at full speed, swooping down on the hapless bird with all the dash of a polo play.

The sheep dipping had gone on three days, and while the days were colorful, the nights had been better. Desert night air near the mountains even in summer is so sharp and clear it hurts. And that natural sharpness thinned the smell of sheep and nicotine, and the drifting smoke from the campfires sweetened it. The campfires were pretty, all over the hills, and Indians sang around them all night long. Whenever anyone felt a romantic urge, there was a Squaw Dance.

The Squaw Dance is an elastic thing. It can be an impromptu affair just for sociability, or it can be quite a ceremony, with a medicine man taking it through in high style. Originally it was a Navaho war dance, but it has lost to a great extent any of that first sacred value. Squaw Dance is the white people's name for it, because the squaws take the lead in the dancing. A woman indicates the partner of her choice by grabbing him firmly by the back pocket of his levis and his belt, and dragging him forcibly into the dance circle. It is etiquette for the man to appear reluctant, but in reality he is highly flattered. At the end of the dance he shows his appreciation by paying the woman. One very dignified visitor at Wide Ruins one night found himself being so taken on, in a moment of impish daring on the part of a squaw, and at the end of the experience he gave her fifty cents. The squaw was surprised, and he himself felt he had overpaid.

Business at the store had buzzed, in its way, during the June wool clips and the July sheep dipping, and it would again in a few weeks, when the traders bought lambs and shipped them out. But Mrs. Beaver with her sacks of wool was more typical of the usual pace of the trading business. Evidently Mrs. Beaver had held back several of her sheep, anticipating some such day as this when she would want a little wool to spend on something extra. They were her sheep, and she could do with them as she pleased. In the Navaho way of life there is no common ownership of property between husband and wife. Each keeps his own property clearly in his own right. This not only makes the Navaho woman one of the most independent on the face of the earth, but it does away with those petty rifts which sometimes arise over the material details of a household.

Mrs. Beaver came sidling into the store, bringing in her flour sacks one by one and stacking them in a corner. Then she sat down on the floor beside them. Bill paid no attention. He knew she had wool to sell, and that her sheep were the long-haired kind whose wool made fine-textured weaving. Moreover, Mrs. Beaver was one of those whom the Lippincotts had managed to educate so far as to sort the wool and wash it, before they brought it in to trade. It would not be the more careless variety which came in little dabs of this and that—long-haired wool and short, a mixture of brown, black, and white, and probably dirty. He knew from experience that Mrs. Beaver had good wool, and that in the end he would pay an especially good price for it. Therefore, he acted completely indifferent. It was no more the politic thing for a trader to be eager to buy than it was for him to be eager to sell. If a trader tried to sell anything to an Indian, the Indian's mind immediately drew warily back and said, "Now wait a minute—" If the trader was so anxious to sell his goods, there must be something the matter with it.

The trading business might lack the strain of Big Business, but nonetheless even its smallest transaction had all the elements of a major fray in collective bargaining. All the canniness on both sides was called into play.

So Bill acted indifferent to Mrs. Beaver's entrance, and on her part, Mrs. Beaver took her wool and sat in a corner with it.

In the next hour Bill sold a leather jacket for a gunny sack full of early pinion nuts. Pinion nuts came in to Wide Ruins by the wagon load, to be shipped out to the eastern markets where in boxes of mixed nuts they turned out to be the little ones always at the bottom. And they came in by the fistful, for a penny's worth of candy.

An Indian named Oscar Whitehair came in and asked Sallie for "ecks." She asked him how many, and he said, "One." She got him one egg, but it seemed that what he wanted was an ax.

John Galeno brought in his clock to set it by the hands on Bill's watch as he had done every morning since their first sale at the store. He hadn't figured it out yet—the steady moving of the little hands around and around to their beginning. But he was still working on it.

Silently Mrs. Beaver got to her moccasins, and made the initial encounter. As a sample of quality and weight, she presented one of the wool sacks, which Bill managed to bump against the counter in the process of taking it from her, to hear how many rocks were in it. It was fairly well loaded. Mrs. Beaver looked blandly off into space. When a point came in the bargaining when it was her turn to make a concession, she'd concede the rocks. But as starter, they both asked for more than they expected to get. Bill offered a price much too low. Mrs. Beaver came back with one equally too high. Nothing coming of that, Mrs. Beaver took her wool sack and sat down again.

Tom Lewis brought in a coyote pelt. A good pelt is worth something, but this was a mangy affair, and Bill gave him only a dollar and a quarter for it. Tom took it out in leather for a neck rein, a bottle of strawberry pop, and a nickel's worth of all-day suckers. A bag of suckers always consummated any deal at the store. But instead of taking his pop and candy outside, as the Indians usually did, Tom hung around the counter, making the pop last a long time before he even started in on the suckers. Obviously Tom had something on his mind. Finally he started talking about the weather. Both Bill and he were surprised it hadn't rained more. Then Tom voiced the opinion

that it would be a better pinion crop this year than last, and
Bill agreed that it looked that way. After a few such pre-
liminaries, the Indian started on what he had come to say. The
pelt had been only an excuse to come and talk. Tom was
puzzled, and troubled.

It seemed that the government this year had cut down on his
grazing permit. Earlier in the month, at the usual yearly
roundup at Wide Ruins, government men had come in and
checked on the number of sheep and horses each family had,
and tallied it with the range conditions for the year, and tried
to make adjustments accordingly.

The Indians do not understand the white man's government.
They know that there is a president, but so far as they are
concerned it is The President—a legendary figure that never
changes. And Washing Done is a complete mystification to
them. Their one real contact with the white people's government was the Head of Indian Affairs, John Collier, but they got
him all mixed up with God, and they didn't think much of
God. They liked Jesus better. Jesus was a shepherd and liked to
keep his flocks, and so do they. The matter of range conservation is utterly beyond them. The government tries to regulate
stock raising scientifically, not only by trying to improve range
conditions by ditches and irrigation, but also in the years when
the herding runs low they ask the Indians to cut down on their
stock—then when the range is built up again, they encourage
the herders to increase their flocks.

But the way the Indians see it is that first of all the government tells them to kill stock, then it tells them to raise stock.
It doesn't make sense, and it discredits the government in their
eyes. Some several thousand years ago the Navahos set one
course for themselves, and they have stuck to it—that of being
horsemen and herders. Furthermore, the middleman who comes
in doesn't always bother to try to explain the government's rea-

son for what to them seems hedge hopping. Sometimes the middleman would merely come in, hold a roundup of the horses and sheep, and order that so many of them be killed, with a peremptory, "John Collier says so."

It is then that the Navahos come to the traders for explanation and advice. They do not understand the government, but they have come to know their traders through daily dealings. So Bill tried to explain the matter of range conservation to Tom Lewis, in terms the Navaho could understand. Tom listened thoughtfully and now and then put in his side of the matter. The talking ironed out some of the wrinkles, but just the same he still thought he ought to be allowed to raise more sheep, and produced a letter he had in his pocket to the agent at Window Rock. He handed it anxiously to Bill to read and address and send for him. All the conversation between the two had been in Navaho, at which Bill had not become master, but he could manage enough of it to carry on his business in the language. But the letter had been written by Tom's daughter who went to school, and was in English. It was divided into four parts:

Part I.

Dear sir,

We had a excess of sheep when we had a permit of Grazine 10 sheep units of livestock on Navaho Reservation. But now I want to know some reasons about.

We can't make a living of only 5 or ten sheep, because I had four children and my wife. That's a large family for only a few sheep. That will do no good. We all want more sheep than ten.

Honestly dear.

Part II.

Please, we are pleasing you very much.

We might be hungry to death this winter, cause we kill sheep for mutton in each week. So that only 10 sheep won't last long to winter.

We want 100 sheeps.

Please I used to work at Fort Wingate job but the roofs fall on me and hurt me badly so I can't work again. Now please let us have 100 sheep on our Grazing Permit. We don't want to be relief by governor. Cause we are shamed of that kind.

I can't stop pleasing you 'til you give me permit of 100 sheep.

Part III.

If you write again back I and my family will go over there and please you and hug you to give us 100 sheep.

If you do what we told you to do we would appreciate it and welcome for it.

We were scarce when we got on 10 sheep unit.

We think only those people who don't have children can have only 10 sheep.

But I had lots of children.

Dearest my agent Please aid me about this.

Don't delay to this friend. Dearest esteem my friend.

Don't you hesitate this.

Reply this letter Friend.

My dear.

Part IV.

We can't make a living like white people cause we can't afford it.

Write by Isabelle Lewis.
Taking message from Tom Lewis.

Bill assured him he would address the letter to Mr. Fryer, the agent at Window Rock, and send it. Tom shook his hand and called him his brother and departed with his potatoes and the one sucker he had left.

Mrs. Beaver again brought up the matter of wool. This time Bill went up a little on his price, and Mrs. Beaver came down, but they still couldn't get together.

Mrs. Patrick Footracer came in the store looking for her husband. She wanted some money. She asked Joe Toddy, who was taking one of his frequent hours off, if he had seen Patrick. Joe said yes, Patrick was around somewhere. But, he begged her earnestly, don't ask him for money today. Patrick was happy today, and when a man's happy, he shouldn't be bothered. He told her to wait and ask for her money tomorrow. Mrs. Foot-racer considered this soberly, finally nodded agreement, and went home, evidently to wait until tomorrow.

Nez Ben's wife came in the store, carrying an unwieldy lot of harness over her arm—carrying it with that splendid disdain which never lets a Navaho woman's work, no matter how drudging, look like drudgery. It was wagon harness and she was bringing it in to pawn. A note from her husband explained matters.

This is Nez Ben.

Today while the sky are blues, I'll make a short request for reasonable. it want to put my harness in pawn for while for ten dollar. We will take it out just the soon this Rug finish. it like to have a shoe and hat. And some more wool. it going to ride tomorrow.

I'll conclude here with my best regarding to you, and many good luckies.

Thank you.

A credit balance for ten dollars went into the books for the new shoes and hat for the jaunty Ben, so he could look his most dashing in the rodeo coming up tomorrow. And Mrs. Nez Ben got her wool so she could go home and work some more at her weaving. Bill would have liked to sell her Mrs. Beaver's wool. But Mrs. Beaver wasn't ready yet.

Presently, however, Mrs. Beaver came forth with a price that was more reasonable. Bill told her that her head was full of wisdom and she was his older sister. He gave her a can of tomatoes. He told her he didn't want to spoil their friendship by too much arguing. He opened the tomatoes for her, added the scoop of sugar the Navahos love, and gave her a paper spoon. Mrs. Beaver went outside to eat her tomatoes and think things over.

Sallie went into the dark room she had made at the back of the store, beside Jimmy's studio, to wash some film. Jimmy was not at his work table that morning. He was up on the hill across the road trailing a rattlesnake track, which was crossing and recrossing itself.

Business had been fairly brisk that morning, but in the afternoon it fell off, and so the traders had a dart game. Mrs. Beaver was back in her corner, not quite persuaded. Crip Chee was in, feeling brash. For a long time he had been outlawed from the store because he had gonorrhea, and wouldn't consent to Bill piling him into the back of the truck and hauling him over to the Ganado hospital for treatment. There was more to Crip Chee's refusal than the usual stubbornness in such cases. Crip Chee's mother-in-law needed to go to the hospital, too, and Bill couldn't see any sense in making two trips when one would do. Crip Chee, however, thought differently, and so did his mother-in-law.

The mother-in-law taboo is a firmly fixed one, and of long standing among the Navahos. As they seem to have recognized early, that is often a ticklish relationship, from both angles. So they cut short the possibility of friction by putting a taboo on the whole idea. A man never stays in the same room with his mother-in-law, nor even comes face to face with her on the open road if he can help it. On her part, the mother-in-law is no more anxious for the meeting than he is. So, everyone being in accord in the matter, when such a meeting seems imminent, a kindly friend will warn one or the other with, "Someone is coming." There never is any question about who that someone is, and the warned one gratefully dodges. So, both the piratical Crip Chee and his mother-in-law, who was something of the same ilk—a woman with a trap mouth and a strange limp— refused to ride together to the hospital. The Lippincotts never had attempted to remodel any of the traditions of the people they had come among, and this seemed no time to start. Nevertheless, they didn't want Crip Chee around, so they exiled him.

Crip Chee would stand off at a distance, his blanket up over his face, and glower—peering out every once in a while to see if the white people were impressed by how angry he was. However, he made no attempt to force his presence upon them and, to the astonishment of the Navahos who knew his ways of old, he sought no violent retaliation for this banishment.

Finally a simple solution presented itself—so simple they wondered they had not thought of it before. Crip Chee rode in the back of the truck facing the rear, and the mother-in-law rode in the front seat. So they rode tranquilly to Ganado back to back, separated from each other by the cab structure. And to further insure herself against the sight of him, the mother-in-law rode with her head completely wrapped in a blanket.

The whole thing was something of an achievement, not only because of the answer to the taboo problem, but because usually patients who needed medical care even very badly had to be almost knocked down and dragged to the hospital. The Navahos around Wide Ruins still had a very definite preference for the healing of the medicine man, through sings and sand paintings. Even the younger ones, who had gone to the white people's schools. They had learned there that their sings and sand paintings were nothing but superstitions, so when they returned to these superstitions they would explain smoothly to the white traders, "We don't really believe in that stuff, but it's cheaper than going to the hospital." The Navaho still was a long way from being a white man's Indian.

But Crip Chee, because the young white people that first day had not shunned and feared him, but laughed with him, went to the hospital for them, once they got it fixed up with his mother-in-law. Now he was back, cured. To show them he held no hard feelings, he stole a watermelon. He slyly picked it up off the counter, hid it under his ragged leather jacket, and sallied over to the pawn department—and tried to pawn it for fifty cents.

A very pretty young Navaho woman came shyly into the store, and stood for a long time at the counter, polishing it slowly back and forth with one dusky palm, before she asked for what she wanted. Then she told Bill Cousins, in Navaho so low he had to bend his head to hear, that she was John Lee's Son-in-law's youngest wife, and her husband had told her she could have four dollars' worth of credit.

Bill Cousins looked surprised. "Why," he told her, "another woman was just in here, and she said *she* was John Lee's Son-in-law's youngest wife. So I've already given away that four-dollar credit."

At that the modest one flew into a blazing-eyed rage. At the discovery that that fickle so-and-so had replaced her in his affections, and so soon, the girl started wearing holes in the floor. The dart shooters hastily withdrew, to give her a broad path. She paced up and down the store floor speaking her mind about John Lee's Son-in-law in terms that made even Crip Chee, who was an expert, listen interestedly. And then she realized that all the Indians on the loafer's bench were doubled over and holding their sides in high glee—and that Bill Cousins was grinning. Finding it was all a joke, and that she still was John Lee's Son-in-law's youngest wife, she began to laugh too. She laughed so hard she had to go over on the bench and sit down.

This matter of the Navaho spreading his favors was an arrangement which seemed quite as acceptable to the women as to the men. Sometimes, of course, there was hair pulled among the younger ones, but in general the women's attitude concerning this rotation was that it gave them more time for their weaving. However, unless the matter happened to come up, as now, it was a system which they did not flaunt before the more complex white society, where the draw between a man and a woman involved the mind and spirit as well as the body.

Even more elemental with them was divorce. A Navaho divorce amounted to no more than the man, or the woman, mounting his or her horse and riding off to some place pleasanter.

The Navahos, who accept simply all natural things, in this seemed to find one form of the fact that all things have a natural conclusion: a time when they end effortlessly because they have fulfilled or exhausted all their active possibilities, and so are ended—quietly, without depth of sorrow cr gladness, but a little of both; enough of both sorrow and gladness to make calm. The end of one thing comes, and, the richer for it, another is begun. But it takes a pristine wisdom to accept endings like that—or else a knowledged clarity which has come through usage.

But when a Navaho starts mixing his simplicities, he is apt to get in trouble, as Mathew Clark did with his alimony. Mathew had been married in white fashion, at least so far as the license. Then when he got tired of his wife, he told her the marriage license had run out and wasn't good any more, and they were divorced. Navaho women not being the kind to go down meekly, Mathew's wife heard about the alimony that went with the white people's divorce, and chased him all around the trading-post yard to get it. She wanted a horse and wagon. She chased him very determinedly, Mathew dodging for his life. Her eyes were snapping fire and she was telling the world her woes at the top of her lungs. Then every once in a while she'd stop and say in a pathetic voice, "I'm just a poor helpless woman." Then she'd take after Mathew again with the shovel.

John Lee's Son-in-law's youngest wife got her four dollars' worth of credit, and the Mifflin came in late in the afternoon and did his very first bit of trading. It wasn't really trading though, because he had a whole dime in cash. He had a terrible time getting up his courage, and finally Joe took him by the hand and led him up to the counter where he proudly and fearfully bought a stick of peppermint candy, and then rushed off without his change.

Just before quitting time, Mrs. Beaver reared herself up for the final encounter. This time she named a price which was about what Bill had figured on paying all along, although it still was a little high. However, he threw off for the rocks, and the deal was made. First of all, with her money, Mrs. Beaver took everything she had out of pawn—a necklace of round silver beads, a couple of bracelets, and a turquoise-studded ring. Also she got out of pawn her shawl—the commercial variety which the Navaho women wear. She bought a hair net. She bought a great many groceries, including several cans of tomatoes, having enjoyed the sample. Bill tried to argue her into putting some of her money into a credit balance for the future. But Mrs. Beaver was all for enjoying her affluence while she had it. As a final fillip, after she had loaded the rest of her trading into her wagon waiting outside, she bought herself three yards of velveteen for a new blouse. She chose the shiny

"Paint and line seemed a sieve through which his experience went."

kind, and blue—which was rank extravagance, because blue fades in the desert sun. The Navahos buy it only for their very best, and Mrs. Beaver departed with it under her arm, with a decided lilt to her moccasined step.

Jimmy had long since found the end of the snake's track he had been following. It had ended in a mouse's hole. He had come into the store, and stood for a time, as usual back out of sight behind the stove, and after a while had gone back to his drawing table. And in the way paint and line seemed a sieve through which all his experience went, and came out clear, Jimmy put design in the day's preoccupations. He had painted steadily all afternoon, and that evening when he had gone and Sallie passed his table on the way to see how her films had turned out, she stopped to see what he had done. On a piece of plain white stationery he had painted three highly colorful snakes whose angling made a pattern. Then on heavy orthodox drawing paper he had done a black and white of a rattlesnake swallowing a mouse, with another mouse standing by, waiting its turn.

Then, in that way suggestion quickened as he worked, the idea of one thing against another went on to be two gray squirrels on the red bend of two boughs, each with a nut. The squirrel with the bigger nut was being avid about it, with the other watching him cunningly. The next picture was of just one of the gray squirrels, with a nut. It was strongly done and hard to say which of the first two squirrels it was.

CHAPTER

12

THE sing to cure Ben Navaho's snake bite was just a small sing. Big and important ceremonies, such as the Mountain Chant, the Night Chant, and the Yeibichei, often lasted for nine nights and days, and were costumed and elaborate affairs. But small sings were almost an everyday occasion. Some family in the Wide Ruins area usually was having a sing, or just had had one, or was going to have one. Sings were a part of their religion, and like all primitives, they governed their whole life by it. The Navaho religion was not a thing set apart—it was not a thing which could be sorted out, and set up, and have it said, "This is their religion." It was the instinctive turn their whole thinking took, or if they got away from it, it was what they came back to. It was the religion of the earth. They drew their life from it, and their resurgent strength when the spirit was ebbing low.

In its organized state, however, the outward ceremonial evidence of their religion took the form of being a curative and preventative measure—which amounted to the same thing. A medicine man would work just as hard to cure a snake bite which might possibly occur, as he would to cure a patient already bitten. Also the time element had nothing to do with the service. Often a sing was held long after the patient was quite well. In this case, Ben had been bitten by a rattlesnake on the left leg, three years before. But it just happened that the idea for a sing and the money for one both happened to hit him at the same time. So word was sent around that there would be a sing at Ben's place, and Ben's family and friends dropped everything and went.

So did the Lippincotts. They closed the store at noon, and took Joe and Jimmy with them.

Ben Navaho's hogan of red-cedar logs sat in the middle of sunbeaten desert, with, a long way off, a rise of earth all around. A few Indian men were loitering around outside, and just beyond the hogan half a dozen women were cooking dinner over an open fire, in an odd assortment of time-old pottery and iron pots, and tin lard cans. There was one wagon with the invariable red water barrel in it, and horses were tethered and quietly standing. In front of the blanketed doorway was a small altar made of a flat, square piece of painted board, and standing behind it was Loukaichukai. Evidently it was a moment of lull in the ceremony, and the old medicine man had come outside to rest. Bill gave him the present he had brought—an abalone shell which he had picked up in a secondhand shop in Gallup. The young traders always kept on the lookout for anything of the sort which the old man could use in his ceremonies. Loukaichukai accepted it with quiet pleasure, and led the way inside, where he added the shell to his medicine basket of fetishes. Sallie kept to the right as she went in, after the manner of Navaho women, and Bill and Joe and Jimmy went to the left and sat down on the floor with the men.

The hogan, which from the outside looked so much a part of the red brown earth, on the inside was a round one-roomed structure of upright logs set to about shoulder height and chinked with red adobe. From there on up juniper logs were crossed and interwoven into a dome, with a sizable hole in the middle for the smoke to go through. But the fire today was not in its customary place in the center of the floor, but instead a small ceremonial fire was burning in front of the door. The door, as do the doors of all hogans, faced east—to greet the sun.

Sallie and Bill were the only white people there, and Sallie the only woman. But there were about twenty men, in overalls and shirts of torn pink, sleazy orange, purple, faded blue. A few had buckskin vests. Some of the younger men had haircuts of indifferent lengths, which they kept back from their faces by bright silk headbands tied in the back. The old men still wore their hair long, in a bundle on the nape of the neck. Everybody wore silver, but only Loukaichukai and John Galeno wore turquoise. The old medicine man wore his usual rich string of it, and John Galeno had a triangle of it hung by a string from the lobe of each ear. John was without his mantel clock today. He had put aside his brooding interest in the repetition of time for an ancient faith that went back beyond his figuring. Today he was leading the chanting for Ben Navaho's sand painting.

Navahos frequently give sand paintings at fairs and exhibitions. But these are sand paintings gotten up for the occasion. The real ceremonies, complete in the detail which makes them sacred, are never enacted for a public spectacle any more than Catholics would hold mass for a curious crowd, or Protestants hold communion. Certain ritualistic acts and chants are always left out or changed for these public affairs, that the rite in its ancient entirety may be kept whole for its original purpose of worship.

The sand painting today, as are all of them in hogans, was being made on the natural sand floor, in the center of the room. It was the Sun and Moon design, one of the most beautiful. Ten men were working on it and it was almost completed. The workers were putting in the rainbows which drew the four sections of the design together—circular lines of blue, rust, and tan, and outlining it in black. The painters were skillfully exact, dribbling the colored sand carefully between their thumb and forefinger.

But the artist working on the section of the design in front of Sallie seemed to have made a mistake. All the other figures in the design—those of the tan eagles and the blue eagles, the gray men and the flying brown squirrel and the gray horse—had feet tipped with arrows. But Loukaichukai made the artist sprinkle some of the natural sand over the feet of arrows he was making, to rub them out. In their stead, under Loukaichukai's direction, he made them of conventional black triangles.

That was one reason why there were so few medicine men on the reservation, because of these colossal feats of memory. Each detail of the ceremonies had to be perfect in itself and in its ordained place in the whole, and undeviating from the way it had been done since the beginning.

Yellow Man was sitting cross-legged at one side of the painting, braiding a necklace which another man was holding for him. The necklace was being made of white corn husks and withes which were soaking in a pan of water to make them pliable. At prescribed places Yellow Man would stick in a feather, or a piece of juniper. It was a pleasant task, evidently, for the two men would stop often to look at it, and measure it, and try it on.

It all was a little like kindergarten—the artists so intent and content at their work, talking occasionally in low tones, now and then laughing a little; borrowing each other's colors. The medicine man stood supervising, pointing out minute changes to be made. Those who were not painting looked on with interest.

When the sand painting was done, the artists got up and crowded in among the other men sitting along the left wall of the hogan. The weavers gave the finished necklace to Loukaichukai, then carefully gathered up every scrap of their materials, and took them outside. When they came back there was no room for them at the left of the hogan, so they sat down beside Sallie, and everybody called low-toned, good-natured jibing to them. Bill, whose Navaho was better than Sallie's, told her they were saying, "Are you women, that you sit on the women's side? So you wear squaw skirts." It was quite a joke for a minute. Then everything grew quiet.

The stage was set, and Ben Navaho came in, a man about fifty but looking not over thirty; not overly tall, but looking strong even under his blanket. Throughout the whole procedure he kept a proud, erect carriage, and his face might have been a face on an old coin. Yet there was an openness to his hauteur, as though he were laying open his spirit to the will of the gods. It was in the way he held his upturned hands, and in the closing of his eyes.

The others who came in to share in the ceremony did not take it quite so earnestly. They were Bent Knee, a gray-mustached man who could have doubled for a cynical man of the world in the movies; an old and harsh woman, and two young women with babies in their arms. Sallie moved over to make room for them, and they sat down in a row beside her. A sand painting costs money—how much depends upon how much the patient can afford to pay. If he can afford nothing, it is given to him free. If he is rich, it seems to take a long time to cure him. But where any money at all is involved, the one who is paying gets the primary treatment, but other members of the family, as now, could come in for some side attention.

Loukaichukai, who had briefly retired, now made his entrance again, dramatically. He came in throwing sacred corn pollen upward into the air, and then down on salient points in the sand design. From his medicine basket he took four flat pieces of painted wood and stuck them into the four corners of the painting, where they stood like gravestones. He added

withes topped with feathers, prayer sticks, a rubber dagger
Bill had once given him. As a last arrangement of the para-
phernalia he made a straight row of containers of herb potions
—a yellow enamel pan, the abalone shell, a pink ten-cent store
cereal dish, half a gourd. Over each of these he sprinkled the
sacred pollen.

That done, John Galeno suddenly closed his eyes, screwed
up his swarthy face in agony, and led off the chanting with a
wild "Hey, ya, ya, ya!" Everybody joined in, except the two
white people and the ones to be healed. While the chanting got
under way, the medicine man was having his patients disrobe.
Ben Navaho took off his blanket, revealing a loincloth of a
chaste piece of flour sacking. Bent Knee's loincloth turned out
to be red and white candy-striped calico. The old woman
glanced scornfully at Sallie and took off her moccasins, hauled
off her blouse, and hoisted her skirts up over her knees. She
had on so many skirts they served sufficiently as loincloth. The
younger women were more modest. They looked at each other
under lowered eyes, and smiled a little. Then slowly they took
off their shoes—children's high-topped shoes: the feet of the
Navaho women are small—pulled up their skirts and shyly
removed their blouses. Then they bent hastily to disrobe their
babies, and when that was done, held their infants before them,
between their breasts. The skin of both mothers and children
was very fair.

For two hours, then, the ceremony went on, to the pulsing
insistence of chanting. The chanting, like the painting in the
sand, was traditionally exact. Three young men sitting together
with rattlers—made of hide shaped when it was wet, and
filled with pebbles and tied to a stick—made the instrumental
accompaniment to the chanting. They sat holding the sticks
loosely in their right hand, so that the shaking motion was
almost imperceptible. They appeared to be paying not the

slightest attention to what they were doing, yet at unpredictable intervals when the whole tempo of the chanting would shift, the rattling would change right along with it, with never a falter or hesitation.

Now and then there were pauses in the chanting, each time different—now stopping in mid air, on a high wail, unexpectedly; now coming with a great guttural letting out of air, like a tire going down. When John Galeno chanted, he kept his ruddy face wrinkled tight, and he swayed and moaned and wailed. Then in the pauses he would open his eyes, wipe the agony off his face, look around and smile, and make some Navaho crack to his neighbor. Now and then Bill got out cigarettes and passed them around, with the men getting up to light the cigarettes at the ceremonial fire.

During all of it Ben Navaho sat with his eyes closed. Now the medicine man was beginning to paint him—using the same colors as those in the sand, except that these came from white clay, red clay, the black from charcoal dust, and the blue from soft ground turquoise. Loukaichukai mixed them as he needed them, on shallow stone palettes, moistening them with water from a tin bucket. Using a quill for a brush, he began with a blue circle on Ben's chest, and from that made a sharp necklace of lightning. The necklace went up over the broad bronzed shoulders—shining from their steaming in the sweat lodge and the sand scouring afterward—down zigzag to a point at the base of Ben's spine. The lines were fine and took a long time.

Occasionally the medicine man stood up and chanted. When the medicine man chanted, everybody else kept still. Then Loukaichukai would bend to his work again. Ben got more lightning, up and down each arm, and down his right leg. On his left leg was painted a snake whose black head ended on his big toenail. The final touch was to his face. It was striped—a broad stripe of tan around his chin, blue across his mouth, gray over his nose, rust across his cheekbones, and copper black over his eyes. He was splendid! And all the time he sat proud and yet submissive, one worthy for the gods to touch.

In the meantime, an assistant who had been called in to help was working on the others. All the dignity and command of presence which was Loukaichukai's, this one lacked. He was a big, loosely put together Indian in dirty pants and a yellow velvet shirt. He had a heavy face and none too good eyes. He had to stop his chanting frequently to spit. The other spitters carefully covered the place with fresh sand, but this one didn't bother. However, he was an expert painter. He put double daubs of black and white, with a rangy thumb and forefinger, all over Bent Knee and the three women and the babies. Bent Knee got tickled when the daubing came to his ribs, and everybody laughed.

The black and white effect proved not unpleasant as it went along—like a snowstorm. Then he undid the women's hair. The old woman let her gray mane hang as it fell. But the two young women draped theirs about them. It fell to their waists and was beautiful. Navaho women take immaculate care of their hair, washing it frequently in yucca suds to make it gleam. Now on each woman a strand of the loosened hair was made to stand straight up, stiff with white clay.

By this time, Ben Navaho was done. The medicine man pulled the rubber dagger from the sand, gave one end of it to Ben, drew him to his feet and led him into the design. Ben sat down carefully in its center, facing the door looking eastward, his feet stretched straight out in front of him, and his hands outheld and open, with proud sanctity to his striped face.

The general chanting stopped, and the medicine man held full sway. He bedecked himself with the corn-husk necklace, throwing it across one shoulder like a bundle of arrows. With that he threw back his head, let out a high wild note from the back of his throat, which seemed to come not from him but from back across the ages. Chanting, then, he started dancing— a high-stepping, smooth-running dance of small steps, with the old man remarkably agile. As he danced he bestowed, one by one, all his ceremonial gadgets upon the patient. He rubbed Ben's chest with them, and touched his feet with them; one of the bundle of feathers proved to have a tin whistle in it, and this he blew around Ben's head like a snake charmer. Several things got tied into Ben's hair—a feather, one of the grave-stone boards; a red string was wound around a strand of hair which was plastered particularly heavily with white clay.

Then he gave Ben to drink from each of the herb potions, after which the helper passed them to the others, each one drinking from the same place in the vessel. The young mothers poured some down the mouths of their babies. What was left, the onlookers reached for eagerly.

This is part of the medicine man's knowledge—the curative power of the roots and herbs and leaves in the desert around him. The Navahos have their own names for them, and this day the white people didn't know whether the dried leaves and seeds, which had been soaking in the medicine bowls while their use was dedicated with prayer and song, were "irritating medicine, itch medicine, gray gummy medicine, or big male medicine." But whatever they were, everyone had some— including themselves. It would have been a breach to have refused it when it was offered. So they took it, and hoped for the best.

The herb vessels emptied, the medicine man sprinkled corn pollen again over the meaningful points in the sand painting, which was pretty well smeared by this time. The final cere-monial destruction of it, however, Sallie did not see. A sand painting is always destroyed after its use, but this a woman

"Symbols of the things that lie behind them—the sun, the sky, the earth, and faith in the Great Spirit."

never sees. The Navaho women dressed, and dressed the babies, and Sallie followed them outside. With them also went Ben Navaho and Bent Knee.

The sun was in its last warmth, and the three Navaho women and the two men stood together, and turned toward it. They stood with lifted faces for a moment. Then, with beautiful motions of their hands they gathered the sun's light unto themselves—the young mothers were lovely the way they brought it over their babies. The others came out from the hogan, and the sand painting for Ben Navaho was over.

As Sallie and Bill were leaving, with Joe and Jimmy coming along behind, Loukaichukai held a detaining hand toward them, and they stopped and waited. The medicine man came up to them, and handed each of them a bundle of the fetishes he had used in the ceremony. As they took them in their hands wonderingly, he said:

"You white people do not believe there is power in these objects."

There was nothing for them to say to that. But after a moment the old man himself went on, in deep-toned Navaho whose sounds seemed to flow and come back to their beginning:

"Nor do I. Any more than that there is power in the images in your churches. These objects merely are the symbols of the big things that lie behind them—the sun, and the sky, and the earth, and faith in the Great Spirit."

Jimmy painted a picture of Ben Navaho's sand painting. It was the only thing he ever did in which there were no animate figures. He painted sage in the wind.

CHAPTER

13

IT WAS October again, and the beginning of their fourth year at Wide Ruins. It was late in the month, and the desert was in its full autumn color. The willows in the bend of the wash from the top of the trading-post hill, looked like a crown laid down for a while.

The Lippincotts were hunting through all their magazines for pictures of Hitler.

A group of Navahos had come into the store and asked, "Who is this Hitler? Want to see his picture."

"Why?"

"Hear lot about him. Must be great feller."

So Sallie and Bill went on a hunt for all the atrocity pictures they could find. When the Indians saw those, they went out from the store ready personally to round up Hitler and kill him. The Navahos of a former age were all warriors. They had placed their force successfully against the Spaniards, the Mexicans, any rival Indian tribe; against America itself. They finally had been subdued only by having their own tactics used against them. They had grown from a handful to a host, by being warriors. But they would present problems to the service ranks of today.

The very preliminary registration questions would be too much for the average Navaho. In the first place, they would be very reluctant to give their real names. In the second, the matter of their age would stymie them completely. Bill had once asked a Navaho, who should have known, how old he was—and the man sat around the store for three days arguing his age with other members of his clan, who might have known. In the end, it was given up as unsolvable. To the question of whether or not they were married, they would be 'apt to say no, since a marriage service never is a necessity and if used at all only for the first marriage. Consequently, their answer to the next question would give pause, since to the query of how many children they had, they no doubt would say ten. Also their utter lack of interest in time would never get them there on the registration day. Altogether, the whole idea of their doing anything about rounding up Hitler seemed doomed to confusion with the very registry attempt.

Still, Joe, as the war in Europe began to get more and more into the talk around the store, was very enthusiastic.

"We used to fought the Apache!" he remembered zestfully. "We used to hide and wait till they went by, then we'd jump on 'em and kill 'em."

If this war involved bush fighting, now, there might be some place for the Navaho in it. But the war was in Europe. However, during the last war in Europe Indians were used to carry messages and phone orders—Tewa, Choctaw, and Navaho had proved indecipherable to the Germans during the last war.

And news of this war, in the fall of 1941, as word of it was getting around by moccasin telegraph over the reservation, began to take fire. From Cozy McSparron at Canyon de Chelley, the Lippincotts heard about the near end of one of the guests over there, at the hands of the Navahos. The latter, loitering in the store, heard the stranger ask directions about going up into the canyon. They listened to an accent with which they were not familiar, and when he had gone asked a ranger who also was in the store what race of man he was. Giving scant attention to the question, the ranger replied, "German."

The Indians stepped outside where they went into a huddle, waved their arms and made noises—and then disbanded in a very purposeful manner. Suddenly the ranger came to with a start, and realized what was going on: the Indians had full plans laid to skirt the canyon trail and ambush the man. They couldn't understand why the ranger told them to stop. The man was a German, the Germans were making trouble, and why not put an end to it?

The Navahos will take a great deal before they interfere, but when the general peace becomes disrupted, then they come together and actively and directly do something about it. In their neighborhood at Wide Ruins, the Lippincotts recently had seen an example of that. There was a man named Harry Dale whose list of crimes was even longer than the loathed and feared Crip Chee's. But the Navahos kept to their policy of noninterference until Harry began adding murder to his list. With that, they went to get him. He was in a sweat lodge taking a bath when he heard them. He heard the pounding of horses' hooves, and tried to get away. The small mound of stone and earth, if difficult for a man to enter even at his leisure, was impossible to get out of in a hurry, and Harry was roped and thrown just as he was crawling out. He bit and scratched and kicked and swore, but they managed to tie him as stiffly with ropes as though he had been stretched out tight on a board. They threw him across the back of a horse and dropped him scornfully on the ground in front of the trading post—ready for the government authorities when they came.

Joe had stood looking at him with a kind of interest. He said that he himself got sent to jail once for ten days, but Lou-kaichukai had held a sing for him, and he got out in three.

When Bill asked what he was sent to jail for, Joe said he had a fight with another Navaho, and shot him twice.

Then he said wistfully, "I missed."

Joe's ineptness with firearms was not typical of all the Navahos, although as a race they probably would not take kindly to organized drill. And they were very vague about the concept of the war. Still, even when they found that it was more than just a matter of every man taking up guns and rabbit sticks and bows and arrows and starting out to clean up, they continued earnestly interested.

The Lippincotts began leaving their magazines out on the store counter for the Indians to look through. Some of them saw a picture of paratroopers in *Life*, and asked about the mechanics of the matter. Although the Navahos will have nothing to do with machinery unless they choose to, nevertheless they usually have a natural aptitude for anything mechanical. So Sallie and Bill got out the bright-colored silk handkerchiefs from the store case, and folded them into parachutes, carefully explaining the operation to intent pupils. Then the traders went up to the flat trading-post roof and sailed the miniature contrivances down—with the Navahos standing below in the yard, looking up and down. A passing car full of tourists stopped, and stared in amazement at two young white people up on a roof, sailing bright-colored toy parachutes down to serious-looking Indians.

The traders put a mason jar on the counter, with a slot in the lid, for contributions toward the China Relief fund. The Mongoloids around Wide Ruins knew about funds. They had had a Christmas fund once, for themselves. Sallie talked to Jimmy about putting in some of the money he was getting from his pictures. Jimmy obediently dropped in a little now and then, but bewilderedly, and without enthusiasm, and the little interest he did have soon petered out. Sallie talked to him again about it, several days later, but he only looked at her, puzzled. So she gave it up and went into the house.

Just as she got inside, there was a terrific roar that seemed to shake the very foundations. Sallie, on her way out, thought about earthquakes and hot-water tanks bursting—then she stopped and looked up. There, zooming back and forth within a few feet of the house, was a beautiful silver army pursuit plane. The tips of the wings and the tail were painted red, white, and blue. She ran and grabbed Jimmy, and joined the crowd which already was milling in the trading-post yard.

Excitement reigned when with one swoop a note shot out of the plane and landed right on the store doorstep. Sallie and Bill already had begun to suspect that the pilot was one of the two who had come to buy a rug and stayed their whole leave—and it was. They waved back at the plane, and the plane dipped its wings in greeting.

In the note was a request for one of Jimmy's pictures. The request mentioned Jimmy by name and said something about the insignia of the diving eagle which Jimmy had made for the pilot when he had been there on his leave. Sallie read that part to Jimmy, and told him to wave at the plane. But the little Navaho boy was so overawed that she had to take his hand out of his pocket and wave it for him.

Joe climbed to the top of the high stone wall which divided the trading-post yard from the house patio, to get nearer the plane, and jumped up and down and yelled, "It's for Jimmy! It's for Jimmy!"

Jimmy decided that a direct order from a soldier in the clouds was not to be trifled with and thereafter he went fifty-fifty with the war relief.

The Navahos were beginning to get something of a clearer idea about the war, as it was thus brought to their desert more actually. Also they were beginning to pick up the talk about

"He spread the sage out in angles, like an open fan."

BEATIEM/AZZ.

the possibility of America getting into it. The old men called a Tribal Council. Sallie and Bill had gone to one of these councils, and the faces of the representatives had been some of the finest they had ever seen. They were not invited to this one, but Loukaichukai was there, and afterward Bill heard what the action of the council members had been. They said that the young men were only beginning to live their lives; they had everything before them. Therefore, the council had decided that if war came, they, the old men, wanted to go in the young men's stead.

Bill tried to explain about age regulations, that young men would be the ones to go.

Then Loukaichukai said if the young men had to go, the old men wanted to go too, so that in actual battle they could go ahead and make it easier for the young ones.

If the Navahos were still vague about the functional details of the war, their spirit was sure. The Navahos have always called themselves proudly The People. It was America who had taken away from them their arrows and their bows, and for this they had returned a scornful hauteur. But now, if war came, The People would be with America in it.

Being a child of the desert, and knowing its violences, Jimmy often had painted one thing attacking another. Now, listening to the war-talk, his painting took that trend increasingly. Attack was the theme, but he was treating it in a new way now. An abstraction was coming into the detail of his paintings. He began trying it out in little ways, touching on the idea lightly. The first experiment was with a piece of green sage on slick paper. He spread the sage out in angles, like an opened fan, and lined it vertically in fine black. It was this abstraction which began to be the interest of his pictures.

On the brown back of a paint pad he did two gnarly night trees with an owl asleep in the branch of one, and a wildcat watching it from the foliage of the other. But the feeling of attack was lost in the trend of the foliage. The green was solid slabs of it, with black check marks for leaves. That particular picture might have been a French primitive.

A mauve panther on a ledge was startling a black horse who had come upon it unexpectedly. But it was the ledge which was of mark—a single red line, which swept onto the gray background and dropped sheer, with the same grace as the green vines which trailed it.

In the picture of a brown bear striking at a yellow lion crouched to spring, there still was viciousness—but it was a tree in the background, the same color as the lion, an abstraction itself, to which the eye was drawn.

Noting the direction Jimmy's work was taking, Sallie thought it was time that he see something of the best of the art which his people before him had done. So she took him to the Southwest Museum at Santa Fe. Joe, who once had gone off the reservation with the Lippincotts, on the memorable trip to Colorado Springs, was as pleased and excited for Jimmy as though he himself were going. He nodded his head vigorously and eagerly to all the preparation plans Sallie tried to make with him about it, although it was plain most of them went over his head. It was to be an overnight trip and Sallie told Joe, in detail, what clean clothes to pack. Joe still was agreeable, but growing vague again, and puzzled.

But Jimmy, who had come to follow his young white friends in everything, followed them out of his desert into the world of cities in unquestioning faith. His literal following of them, at about a distance of ten paces behind, was slightly disconcerting on the sidewalks of Santa Fe. Sallie would listen, and pick out from the hurrying of other footsteps, the clumping of his heavy yellow shoes trudging faithfully along behind, and

"There still was viciousness, but it was a tree to which the eye was drawn."

knew he still was there—until they came to a flight of stairs, just inside the hotel. Sallie started on up, and then realized there was no longer the clump of the yellow shoes behind her. She turned and looked back. And there at the bottom of the stairs, the little Navaho boy, who had come from a sand country where there were no steps to climb, had stopped. But he was hanging on tightly with both hands to the wrought-iron railing, looking up at her intently. He could see what she did with her right foot, but he couldn't figure out what she did with her left! So Sallie went on, more slowly, to show him.

When they got to his room, she said, "Jimmy, may I look in your suitcase, to see if you have everything you need?"

"Yiss—" whispered Jimmy. Then he cleared his throat. "Yiss—" he said again, a little louder—and ducked his head, and he grinned that grin of his.

Sallie opened the bag, which was a tremendous one. As she had suspected, any suggestions about clothes beyond the outer essentials had been completely incomprehensible to Joe. But folded very neatly in a small pile and tied to the middle of the bag were shirts and socks, and set squarely on top of them was a toy silver gun with a pearl handle and cowboys carved all over it which Bill had once given Jimmy.

She showed the little boy from the desert of hogans about the bathroom fixtures, and turned down the bedclothes for him. He watched and listened carefully, and the next morning obviously none of it had been touched. But there was a pillow on the floor. Jimmy often lay on the Lippincotts' library floor at Wide Ruins, with a pillow under his head, holding an ice pack, or a boric pad, to a black eye after one of his fights. Sallie asked the maids not to disturb him, for that, she knew, would have been too much. Nevertheless, the little boy went through the hotel experience, after he had mastered going up the stairs, with apparent perfect composure. In the dining room, if Sallie took a drink of water, Jimmy took a drink of water. When she picked up a fork, so did he.

She had chosen six of his paintings for him to bring along and present to the museum. There was quite a to-do over them, but the boy who had painted them paid not the slightest attention. He was completely absorbed with the findings he was making in the work of his ancestors. He was shown the rarest old chief blankets the museum had—their colors mellowed and richened with the years, but still true. He stood engrossed before them, inquiring into the patterns of this former age—patterns with an abstraction which a long-ago people had put into their art for themselves and their seed. He stood before wide bands of silver, with an angularity to their design so modernistic Picasso himself might have done them. That was what Sallie had wanted him to see—that the abstract trend his own little drawings were beginning to take of themselves, was a reaching back to the ways of his fathers.

He said nothing. But his dark eyes were big, and the morning after they arrived home Joe came in to fix the house fires looking as though he had not slept. But he was blissful.

"Jimmy talk all night long."

The little boy who had made his father sad because he never talked to him, had grown suddenly articulate. It was a proud heritage which the little Navaho boy had been brought to see.

CHAPTER

14

FOR the first Saturday in December it was exceptionally warm. The wind blew and the sun was patchily bright.

It was too fine a day to stay indoors and, as they always did when anything better to do came along, Bill shut up the store. Had Bill Cousins been there, he would have left the running of it to him, of course. But the clerk was in California—his first trip off the reservation where he had been born into the trading business. So Bill cleared out the customers, and told them he'd be back after a while. The Indians would wait. Indians weren't in any hurry.

"Get 'em oop da hawrses?" wondered Joe, at seeing Bill leaving the store an hour before lunch was due.

"And put the saddles on Creed and Pantywaist." They still had to be explicit about that, or they'd find themselves riding Joe's Dotse.

"Uh huh," grunted Joe, and shuffled off up toward the corral as though he supposed they were riding the horses they wanted to, but all he could say to that was that their judgment was poor.

They rode up through the familiar washes, over rocks they had come to know, whipped around pinion branches they had learned to avoid, and came up to a high place. The horses were breathing heavily, and they pulled up and stopped, to rest and to take a look across.

The air was soft-winded, and the mountains beyond looked

misty and right. There was an odd fullness, a repose to every-thing. It was a wide and peaceable land they looked on, of sun and quiet, with the quiet loved fiercely, as never before, in the threat to it.

The ride back was wild, with Creed taking the lead in leap-ing the final ditch up to the corral hill, and Pantywaist plung-ing close on his heels.

Walking down from the corral to the house they went by the swimming pool, where Loukaichukai was sitting on the terrace. The terrace around the pool was part of the original ruins of Kintiel—and Indians had been sitting on that terrace for nearly two thousand years. The old medicine man was sitting there reading. Loukaichukai's first call upon them had been formal to the extreme. But now he called often, and would stay a while. He liked to look at the Lippincotts' mag-azines. His favorite reading was *The New Yorker*, which he always read upside down. As they went by, he looked up in greeting and his eyes warmed, then he bent earnestly again to the cartoon at hand. He studied it thoroughly, then solemnly turned the page to the next one, upside down.

Although it was warm out in the sun, fires were needed in the house. Joe had built them up while they were gone, and when they came back in, there was crackling from fireplaces all over the house, and a smoky fragrance. It smelled like a brand new lead pencil, with just a dash of lemon. The partic-ular illusiveness of that smoke of pinion and juniper burning together was one of the first things they had remembered about this part of the country. It was one of those small things that ties you to a place.

Also, mingling in with the smell of wood fires was the spicier one of ginger cookies. It was a recipe the cook had picked up in the winter of '28.

"How about some of those ginger cookies, Bess?"

Bess had just recently acquired a permanent. She had come back from her last day off in Gallup with her straight black Indian hair in kinks. In time it would loosen up, but meanwhile she was very proud of it.

"Fifteen minutes till loonch," Bess told them flatly, in the matter of ginger cookies.

"We don't care."

"Fifteen minutes!" warned Bess, her harsh voice swinging up on it.

"Ginger cookies!"

Bess swished into the kitchen, banging open the door, and reappeared with a terrific plate of them. There was a small commotion in the library, where Jimmy worked now, under the windows. Sallie and Bill looked in at the door and asked him what he was doing. There was sudden silence, and they went in to see.

He was sitting at his drawing table, his heels hooked over the chair rung, and his head bent over the painting he was finishing. It was of a blue horse. An arrogant creature, with all that Jimmy had been given to inherit put into it with new freedom and force. Fan-shaped sage and a gnarl of a tree made abstract detail. Then by a light yellow outline like sunlight over everything, the little boy was giving the whole an odd lift. A blue horse, if the world got tired.

When they looked, in a silence that grew full, from the blue horse to the little boy, he turned his dark head around almost backward to hide his shy smile for them. The small commotion had just been his moving the paints a little nearer. But he wouldn't say so. After a moment though, when they offered him some ginger cookies, he had some with them. The cookies were the old-fashioned kind, big and substantial. Just as they had managed the last one, Bess charged the door. She eyed the empty plate brightly, and then arched her black brows in triumph.

"Loonch," she announced, "is sarved."

It was so warm, they had it outdoors in the patio.

"Whatchoo want to drink?" wondered Bess, standing beside them and swinging her arms. "Coca-Cola, root beer, lemon pop, or sarsaparilla?"

"Coca-Cola," said Bill, for a change. Then he tasted it, and looked up at the maid. "This is pure syrup. I don't want it that strong. Put a little water in it."

"Seezy!" said Bess. But she laughed, with that toss to it.

Bess still had her little ways. When Sallie would correct her about something, Bess paid no attention. She appeared not to hear. But about an hour later she would come sallying in with a cheerful, "I sure did that wrong, didn't I?"

"You got company," she announced now.

It was Mr. Parquette. The Lippincotts rose to greet him, glad to see him. They hadn't see him since he had left for Mexico.

Mr. Parquette looked around at the patio, and missed the familiar pile of tin cans and cartons.

"If I'd knowed you wanted that stuff hauled out of here, I could have done that for you," he said, about the changes that had been made.

They laughed, and said, "Come have lunch with us."

Mr. Parquette didn't care if he did, and they asked him how Mexico was.

"I liked it real well," acknowledged Mr. Parquette. "I'm glad to be back though."

"Did you get all that thrill you're supposed to, when you set foot in your own country again?" wondered Sallie.

"Well," said Mr. Parquette, "no. Oh, it was interesting, coming into El Paso. But it was just like another foreign city. I didn't really feel like I was home until I crossed the county line."

Which reminded him. "Say, you folks ever go to the county seat and get those records straightened out about your hundred and sixty acres?"

"What hundred and sixty acres?"

"Didn't I tell you?" said Mr. Parquette. "There's a hundred and sixty acres goes with Wide Ruins."

"Where?"

Mr. Parquette waved a hand in the general direction of the horizon. "There—"

After lunch they got excitedly into the car and drove to the county seat to look up the exact location of their newly found hundred and sixty acres. Mr. Parquette rode that far with them, on his way back to Gallup, where he looked forward to spending the rest of his days contentedly standing on the street corner, his red bandanna knotted at its four corners to make a hat, and watching the world go by.

The clerk at the courthouse was a dusty little man, who put on his spectacles obligingly and got out the files for them. He found a lot of mighty interesting and well-written records—which he read aloud to them—but they weren't theirs. Then he came across a picture of his wife and himself, taken on their wedding day. He was sitting in a photographer's chair in his checked wedding pants and a shirt which he remembered nostalgically as being purple. He was holding his sombrero stiffly in his hand, and stiffly in front of his bride, who was standing just back of his chair beside him, was a bunch of flowers which she was holding at arm's length.

The clerk was so moved by the discovery that nothing would do but they all go over home with him and meet the wife.

Then they trooped back to the courthouse, and went through some more mighty interesting records which weren't theirs—

and this time got interrupted by a young couple who came in to be married. The clerk read the service, and Sallie and Bill stood up with them. They were a country couple. The girl was not exactly pretty, but she went through the brief civil ceremony with a clear, sure kind of happiness on her face which made it so. She seemed not to be thinking, exactly, of the words she was hearing, but a sense of rightness pervaded her answers. She went through her wedding with a light, sure joy. She reached about shoulder height to the boy, who stood looking down at her with a sober, almost stern kind of care.

When they had gone, it was still for a minute in the court-house. Then the clerk briskly took off his glasses and wiped them, and suggested they all go have a drink to the bride and groom. By the time that was done, the courthouse was closed.

In the evening, on their way back to Wide Ruins, coming along the sand road toward them, they saw Joe and Jimmy. Joe waved joyfully, and they stopped the car. Joe was glad to see them. He knew Bill was joining the Navy and he had been afraid, when they had gone off so suddenly and been so long, that maybe he'd left for good. And he and Jimmy had started out to meet Sallie, if she should be coming back alone. The handy man already had assured Bill he would take care of Wide Ruins for him while he was gone. And he had told Sallie that he and Loukaichukai would hold a sing, and pray all night on the hill. Joe had come to them once in time of need, about Mary, and they had been his friend. Now he would be their friend. But he was relieved to see that his time of proving hadn't come yet, and that Bill was still around, and they all shook hands on it. Jimmy, as always, promptly had ducked out of sight around the corner of the car, but Sallie held out a hand in his general direction, too, and after a minute she felt a warm, strong little hand slide shyly into hers.

Then Joe and Jimmy got in the car, and they drove back to

Wide Ruins together. From the top of the hill, looking down into the shallow valley which sheltered the trading post, the old stone buildings seemed held in the hollow of a hand, like a dream made certain. The house lights were on, and looked so welcoming.

After they had put the car away, Sallie and Bill stood a moment, in the yard. There was a quarter moon, just enough to throw their shadows faintly, and the night sky around it was so rich a blue it seemed to have copper in it. But around the edges the sky was very light. They still hadn't found out exactly where their boundaries lay. Mr. Parquette had just waved a hand toward the horizon, as theirs. And for Jimmy there was the blue horse.